EQUAL LOVE

EQUAL LOVE

STORIES

PETER HO DAVIES

A MARINER ORIGINAL

HOUGHTON MIFFLIN COMPANY

BOSTON · NEW YORK

2000

For information about permission to reproduce selections from
this book, write to Permissions, Houghton Mifflin Company,
215 Park Avenue South, New York, New York 10003.

Library of Congress Cataloging-in-Publication Data

Davies, Peter Ho, date.
Equal love / Peter Ho Davies.
p.   cm.
"A Mariner original."
ISBN 0-618-00699-0
I. Title.
PR6054.A89145 E68   2000
813'.54—dc21   99-046755

Book design by Anne Chalmers
Typefaces: Janson Text, Akzidenz Grotesk Extra Bold Condensed

Printed in the United States of America

QUM 10 9 8 7 6 5 4 3 2 1

The following stories have appeared, sometimes in slightly different
form, in these publications: "The Hull Case" in *Ploughshares*; "The
Next Life" in *Harper's Magazine*; "How to Be an Expatriate" in *Grand
Tour* and *Prospect Magazine*; "Frogmen" in *Fish Stories*; "Sales" in *Third
Coast*; "Everything You Can Remember" in *Granta*; "On the Terraces"
in *The Gettysburg Review*; and "Today Is Sunday" in *The Atlantic Monthly*.

FOR LYNNE

For Lynne

"For a wonderful physical tie binds the parents to the children; and — by some sad, strange irony — it does not bind us children to our parents. For if it did, if we could answer their love not with gratitude but with equal love, life would lose much of its pathos and much of its squalor, and we might be wonderfully happy."

— E. M. Forster, *Where Angels Fear to Tread*

ACKNOWLEDGMENTS

For support during the writing of this book, I would like to thank the Fine Arts Work Center in Provincetown; Emory University; the University of Oregon; and my friends and colleagues at all three institutions.

For their expertise, faith, and encouragement, I'm greatly indebted to Janet Silver and Heidi Pitlor at Houghton Mifflin and Maria Massie and Joshua Greenhut at Witherspoon Associates.

Finally, for their unequaled love, my deepest thanks go to my family.

CONTENTS

EQUAL LOVE

EQUAL LOVE

Of modern North American cases, one of the earliest and
most widely reported abductions occurred in the early sixties to a mixed-race couple in New Hampshire.

—*Taken: Twelve Contemporary UFO Abduction Narratives,*
K. Clifford Stanton

HELEN IS TELLING the col-
onel about the ship now, and Henry, sitting stiffly on the sec-
tional sofa beside his wife, can't look up. He stares at the
colonel's cap, the gold braid on the rim, where it rests on the coffee table next to the latest *Saturday Evening Post* and the plate of
tunafish sandwiches Helen has laid out.

"What color were the lights, Mrs. Hull?" the colonel wants to
know, and Helen says, "Blue."

The colonel makes a check mark.

"Baby blue," Helen adds. She looks at Henry, and he nods
quickly. He thought the lights were a cop at first.

"Baby blue," the colonel repeats slowly, his pen scratching
along. He's resting his clipboard against his khaki knee. His
pants leg is crisply ironed, and his shoes glint. Henry wishes he
could see what the colonel is writing.

"Is that usual?" he asks. "Blue lights? In these cases, I mean."

"I'm afraid I couldn't say," the colonel says.

" 'Cept I believe aircraft lights are usually red and white."

"Yes, sir."

"Then this wouldn't be an aircraft?"

"That's what we're aiming to determine," the colonel says.
"Sir." His smile reminds Henry of Richard Widmark.

There's a pause, and then Helen asks, "Won't you have a sand-wich, colonel?" and the colonel says, "Thank you, ma'am. Don't mind if I do." He takes one and lays it on his plate, but doesn't take a bite.

Henry thought the lights were a cop at first. They'd al-ready been stopped once on the drive back from Niagara. He could have sworn he'd been doing less than sixty. The cop had shone his flashlight in Henry's face—black—and then Helen's—white.

"Any trouble here, ma'am?"

"Not at all, officer," she told him, while Henry gripped the wheel with both hands.

•

It was meant to be a second honeymoon. Not that they'd had a first, really. They'd been married for seven years. Henry had been serving in Korea, a corporal in the signals, when he'd been caught in the open by a grenade. Helen was his nurse in Tokyo. He'd heard that some of the white nurses refused to touch the black GIs, but she didn't mind. The first day she gave him a sponge bath, he tried to thank her—not sure if he was more em-barrassed for her or himself (he felt an erection pushing at the slit of his pajama pants)—but she told him not to be silly. He al-ways remembered that. "Don't be silly." Like it was nothing.

"I'm just saying I appreciate it," he said, a little stung. "The nature of the race matter and all."

"The race matter doesn't matter to me," she told him briskly. "And it shouldn't matter to you." Later she came back and he asked her to scratch his back, below the shoulder blade where it itched him fiercely, and she did.

Perhaps it was the thought of losing his arm. He was so relieved when she told him they'd saved it. She'd been changing
the dressing on his hand, unwinding the bandages from each fat
finger. He whooped with joy. He asked her to have a drink with
him. She said she didn't think so and his face fell, but then she
laughed, her teeth as bright as her uniform. "Oh," she said, turning his hand over to wash it. "You mean after your release? Why,
of course. I'd like that. I thought you meant now. You shouldn't
be drinking now, not with your medication." And then she
wound his hand up again in fresh white bandages.

Her tour had finished three weeks later, but she'd stayed on in
Tokyo, and by the time his discharge came through, they were
lovers. They ate sushi together and she wore beautiful multi-
colored kimonos and it all seemed perfectly natural. He'd been
in the army for nine years, so he hung on to her now as the next
thing in his life, and one night after a fifth of whiskey—"Why,
Henry Hull, you're stinko"—he asked her to marry him. "Of
course," she said, and he laughed out loud. "*Of course!*" They'd
gone back to New Hampshire, where she had a job in a hospital
in Manchester. He'd found work at the local post office, and
they'd been married within the month.

They'd made a good life together. Helen's parents had been
kind to him, after some reservations. "They know better than to
try and stop me when I want something," Helen told him. Her
brother called Henry a hero and a credit to his race at the small
reception after their wedding at the town hall. Henry appreciated it, but it only reminded him that he was the one black man
in the room. His own parents were long since dead, and his sister, Bernice, back in Summer Hill, had refused to come when
she heard Henry was marrying a white woman. "What for?" she

wanted to know, and when Henry said, "For the same reasons anybody gets married," she told him no, she didn't believe it.

Henry didn't know what to say to that. He could hear her kids, his nephews and nieces, in the background, yelling, and then a baby's sharp, sudden sobs.

"I gotta go," Bernice said. They hadn't talked since.

His brother, Roy, had been more sympathetic. "You and me been dreaming about white girls since we were boys. Bernice thinks that's all wrong and maybe it is, but a man's got to follow his dream. 'S only natural to want what you can't have." But Roy hadn't come either.

Henry and Helen did have a good life, though. Decent friends. Enough money. Helen had even taught him to skate. He liked his job, was proud of the uniform, and Mr. Rhodes, the postmaster, treated him well. The first week, when there'd been a little trouble over Henry's eating at the local sandwich shop, Mr. Rhodes had stepped across the street and told the owner that none of the postmen would be eating there again if Henry didn't. And just like that the shop integrated, although Henry told Helen he wouldn't have made anything of it himself.

"Why not, for Pete's sake?" she'd asked him, and when he shrugged she'd exclaimed, "You're too darned dignified for your own good sometimes."

He was the only black man he knew in Manchester, but he followed the news of lunchroom sit-ins and the Freedom Riders and joined the NAACP, although he was a lifelong Republican, like his father and his grandfather before him. He met more Negroes, but they all seemed a little shy of each other, almost sheepish. "Far as civil rights goes," one of them pointed out to him, "New Hampshire ain't exactly where it's *at*."

What nagged Henry was that it was all too good, unreal

somehow, more than he deserved. He thought of his brother and sister and all the kids he'd grown up with. Why had he been the one singled out, plucked up by life and set down here? It made him a little scared to have something. Helen said he was just being superstitious, but he couldn't shake the idea. He thought one day he'd wake up, or someone would come along and take it all away. When Helen had miscarried the first time, the spring before, along with the worry for her, he'd felt an awful relief that finally something terrible had happened. He'd been so ashamed he hadn't known how to comfort her, except to keep trying. But when she'd miscarried the second time, that summer, he'd decided they couldn't go through it again. They'd been distant these last few months, Helen insisting she still wanted a child, had always wanted one, Henry doubtful, thinking *She wants one more now she maybe can't have one*, wondering if this was how she had once wanted him, wondering if he was no longer enough for her, which was why the idea of a trip to Niagara felt like such an inspiration.

Helen had laughed and called him a romantic but taken his hand across the dinner table.

•

The colonel wants to go back over the details again, as if he's trying to trip them up. "I thought you said it was cigar-shaped, Mrs. Hull?"

"From a distance," Helen says impatiently. "Up close, you could see it was a disk." She looks at Henry for support.

"We had a pair of binoculars along for the trip," he says. "I thought it might be a star at first. But when I pulled over at a lookout and used the glasses, whatever it was was definitely moving." The colonel is silent, so Henry hurries on, a little breathless but feeling that more is required of him. "A little later it came to me that I'd left the car running the first time while I leaned on the roof with the binocs. I thought the vibrations from the engine might have been the problem, see, so I pulled over again, stepped away from the car before I put the glasses on it. And it was still moving."

Henry wants the colonel to write this down, but his pen doesn't move. The colonel doesn't even ask him about the binoculars—his service issue 10×42 Weavers.

"Spinning," Helen says. "Don't forget it was spinning. That's what gave it the twinkling effect."

"Right," Henry says. "The lights that looked like they were moving across it from a distance were actually fixed to the rim." He makes a circling motion in the air with his index finger while the colonel stares at him.

"Did you write that down?" Helen asks, and the colonel blinks and says, "Yes, ma'am. I got it. 'Twinkling was spinning.' "

They had agreed before the colonel arrived that Helen would do most of the talking. Henry hadn't wanted them to tell anyone about what they had seen right from the start, but Helen insisted on calling her sister, Marge. Hadn't Marge seen a UFO herself in '57? Henry shrugged. He'd never believed Marge's story, but he knew Helen needed to tell someone, and Marge at least wouldn't make fun of them. But it hadn't stopped there. Marge put Helen on to a high school science teacher she knew, and he told her they should really notify the air force. Now here was the colonel with his clipboard. Henry hadn't wanted to meet him, but Helen had had a conniption fit.

"Henry Hull! How's it going to look," she said, "if I'm telling this story and my own husband won't back me up?"

Henry told her it wouldn't make any difference, but what he really thought was that nothing he said would help her, might even make her less believable. "You're a white woman married to a colored," he wanted to tell her. He didn't think anyone would believe them, but Helen wasn't having any of that. "Of course they'll believe us," she said. "So long as we tell the truth. We have to try, at least. You've no gumption, Henry, that's your whole trouble." It seemed so easy to her, but Henry had had to work hard to be believed most of his life.

Now he can see that Helen is getting tired of going over the same story again and again.

"I'm not telling you what it means," she says. "I'm just telling you what I saw. We were hoping *you* could explain it to *us*."

But the colonel just spreads his hands and says, "Sorry, ma'am."

"You act like we're lying."

"No, ma'am," the colonel says quickly. "I assure you."

Henry knows what's coming next. Helen wants to get on to the part inside the ship, the stuff Henry doesn't remember. He asked her not to talk about it, but she told him she couldn't promise. "What if it's a matter of national security?" she said. "It's our duty, isn't it? Think what it could mean for the future of everyone." So now she explains to the colonel how she only remembered this part later, in her dreams. Henry feels himself shrink, but the colonel just makes another scratch with his pen, and Helen starts to tell him about the aliens—the short gray men—and their tests.

"Gray?" The colonel looks from Helen to Henry, Henry to Helen.

"Gray," she says, and he writes it down.

"And short," she adds. "But not like dwarfs, like children."

In her dream, Helen says, she remembers them scraping her skin with a strange metal instrument. "Like a dentist might use, only different. It tickled," she recalls, without a smile. Then she remembers them pushing a long thin needle into her navel. "That really hurt," she says, "but when I cried out they did something and the pain stopped at once. They seemed sorry. They told me it was a pregnancy test."

The colonel, who has been taking notes with his head down, not looking at them, glances up quickly.

"Oh, of course I'm not pregnant," Helen says brusquely, and Henry sits very still. This is what he feared all along—that they wouldn't be able to keep their private business out of this.

"Have you ever heard of anything like it?" Helen asks. The colonel tells her he hasn't.

"You have no memory of this?" he asks Henry, who shakes his head slowly. He's racked his brains, but there's nothing. Helen can't understand it. "How can you not remember?" she cried the first time she told him, as if he were the one being unreasonable.

"Helen tells me I was in another room on the ship, drugged or something, but I don't recall." He wishes he could support her now, but also, in the back of his mind, he resents her dream, his weakness in it.

Helen presses on. She says she knows how it sounds, but she has proof. "I'm just getting to the best part," she says. "The part about Henry's teeth."

"Teeth?" the colonel says, and this time Henry sees a twitch to his lips that makes him feel cold inside.

"That's right," Helen says, and Henry can tell she's seething now. The aliens, she explains slowly, as if to a child, were surprised that Henry's teeth came out and Helen's didn't. "They didn't understand about dentures," Helen says. Henry feels his mouth grow dry. They have argued about this part. He didn't want her to tell it, but Helen feels it's the clincher. "How could we make that up?" she asked him last night. "Plus there's the physical proof."

"This was after the other tests," Helen says. "They were as curious as kids. I'm jumping ahead a little, but don't mind me. Anyway, after we were done, the one I think of as the doctor, he left the room, and the *grayer* one, the leader, he told me they were still finishing up with Henry. Anyhow, a few seconds later the doctor runs back in. He seems very excited and he asks me to open my mouth. Well, I don't quite know why, but I wanted to get this over with, so I obliged, and before you know it he'd pushed his little fingers in my mouth and he was pulling on my teeth. Well! You can imagine my surprise. I slapped his hand away quick as I could. He was pulling quite hard too, making my head go up and down. 'What do you think you're doing?' I said, and then he held out his other hand, and can you guess what he had?"

The colonel shakes his head slowly.

"Why, Henry's dentures. There they were, sitting in his little gray hand. Well, I snatched them up at once. I don't know what I was thinking. It made me so worried about Henry, I guess. That and the fact that he's always losing them, or pretending to lose them, anyway."

She pauses, and Henry thinks he should say something.

"They pinch me," he mumbles. "And they click. I don't like them so good."

Helen laughs. "I tell him he looks like a fool without them, but he doesn't care. He has such a fine smile, too."

Henry looks past the colonel's shoulder and out the picture

window. He does not smile. It's October, and the first snow is beginning to fall in the White Mountains.

"Anyway, I snatched them up, and then the leader started in about why my teeth were different from Henry's, so I had to explain all about dentures, about how people lose their teeth as they get older or, like Henry here, in accidents. I thought it was funny they were so flummoxed by dentures, but you know, now that I come to think about it, I don't remember seeing their teeth. They had these thin little slits for mouths, like I said before, and when they talked it was as if they didn't move their lips."

"Did they speak English?" the colonel asks. "Or was it more like telepathy?"

"Maybe," Helen says. "Like voices in my head, you mean? That certainly could explain it."

"And their fingers?" the colonel asks seriously. "Would you say they had suckers on them? Small pads maybe?"

Helen pauses and looks at him hard. "No," she says very clearly. "I would have remembered something like that."

There is an awkward pause before she goes on more brightly.

"Anyway, to cut a long story short, I thought the whole thing about the dentures was funny and I remember laughing, but it must have been one of those nervous laughs, because afterward when I looked at my hand where I'd been gripping them, I'd been holding them so tight that the teeth had left bruises." And here Helen holds out her hand to the colonel. He leans forward and takes it and turns it to the light. Henry can just see the crescent of purpling spots in the flesh of her palm.

Helen nudges him. Henry doesn't move for a moment, but then he decides. She's his wife. He'll try to help. He holds a handkerchief over his mouth and slips his plate out. He passes it

to her, and with her free hand she places it in her palm so that
the false teeth lie over the bruises. The denture glistens wetly,
and Henry looks away in embarrassment.

"See," Helen says triumphantly. "Now that's evidence, isn't
it?"

"It's something, ma'am," the colonel says, peering at Henry's
teeth. "It's really something."

•

Henry has tried his damnedest to remember what Helen's talking about. But he can't do it. It's the strangest thing, he thinks,
because he recalls the rest of the trip — start to finish — vividly.

They'd gotten up at five A.M., packed the car, and been on the
road to Niagara by six. Henry wanted to get a good start on
the day. It was September, peak foliage. "What impossible col-
ors," Helen breathed, sliding across the seat to lean against him.
"Better than Cinerama," he told her. He'd sung a few bars of
"Oh, What a Beautiful Morning" and made her laugh, and she'd
done her best Dinah Shore: "Drive your Chev-ro-lay, through
the U.S.A." She'd got impatient with him the evening before for
simonizing the car, bringing out the gloss in the two-tone paint
job. Now, he saw, she was proud.

But when they stopped for brunch at a diner in upstate New
York, Henry felt uneasy. The din in the place died when they en-
tered, and the waitress seemed short with them. He ordered coffee and a doughnut, but Helen had the short stack and took her
time over her coffee. When he called for the check, she looked
up and asked what his hurry was, and he said they still had a ways
to go. Didn't he know she had to let her coffee cool before she
could drink it? "Have a refill or a cigarette," she said, pushing
the pack of Chesterfields across the table, but he told her a little

sharply he didn't want either. He felt people watching him. Helen finished her coffee and went to the bathroom, leaving him alone for five long terrible minutes. He could hear a child crying somewhere behind him, but he didn't turn to look. When she came back he hurried her out before she could retie her scarf, leaving a big tip. He had to stop to urinate fifteen minutes later and she made fun of him for not going earlier. "You're like a little boy," she said, and so he told her how he had felt in the diner.

"Oh, Henry," she said. "You were imagining it."

It made him mad that she wouldn't believe him, wouldn't take his word for it, but he didn't want to spoil the trip with a fight and he let her half convince him, because he knew it would make her feel better. He played with the radio, pushing buttons until he found some Harry Belafonte. Helen just didn't notice things the way he did. He loved her for it, this innocence, cherished it, though he couldn't share it (found his own sensitivity sharper than ever, in fact). That night when he stopped at two motels and was told that they were full, he didn't make anything of it, and when she said as they left one parking lot, "You'd think they'd turn off their vacancy sign," he just let it ride.

"Must be a lot of lovers in town," she added, and squeezed his thigh.

When they finally found a room at a place called the Falls Inn, she pulled him to her and he started to respond, but when she told him she'd forgotten her diaphragm, he pulled away.

"It'll be okay," she told him. "Just this once." She clung to him for a moment, holding him against her, before he rolled off. They lay side by side staring at the ceiling as if it were the future. After the second miscarriage, Helen had been warned that she might not be able to carry a baby to term. "We can't take the risk," Henry told her softly, but she turned away. "You're afraid," she said, curled up with her face to the wall. The knobs of her spine reminded him of knuckles. "I'm afraid of losing you," he said at last.

He told her he'd go out and get prophylactics, but driving around in the car, he couldn't. He stopped outside one store and sat for fifteen minutes, waiting for the other cars in the lot to leave, listening to the engine tick as it cooled. He *was* afraid of losing her, he knew, though the admission, so abject and ineffectual, shamed him. But behind that fear was another — a dim, formless dread of his own children and what they might mean for the precarious balance of his marriage, which made him shudder. There was one more car in the lot, but before it left a police cruiser pulled in, and Henry backed out and drove slowly back to the motel.

When they were first married, Helen used to call him by a pet name, Big, burying the tight curls of her permanent against his chest. He would stroke her neck and answer in the same slightly plaintive baby talk, "Little" or "Little 'un." It was how they had comforted themselves when they felt small and puny beside their love for each other, but remembering it now only made him feel hopeless before the childlessness that loomed over them. Helen was asleep when he got in, or pretending, and he lay down beside her as gently as possible, not touching but aware of her familiar warmth under the covers.

The next day had started better. They'd gone to the falls and been overwhelmed by the thundering white wall of water. They bought tickets for the *Maid of the Mist*. Henry bounced on the springy gangway and made her scream. They laughed at themselves in the yellow sou'esters and rain hats the crew passed out and then joined the rest of the identically dressed crowd at the bow railings. "Oh look," Helen said, pointing out children, like miniature adults in their slickers and hats, but Henry couldn't hear her over the crash of the falls. "Incredible," he yelled, leaning forward, squinting in the spray as if in bright light. He could taste the mist in his mouth, feel the gusts of air displaced as the water fell. Suddenly he wanted to hold his wife, but when he turned to Helen, she was gone. He stumbled from the railing looking for her, but it was impossible to identify her in the crowd of yellow slickers. He felt a moment of panic, like when she'd left him in the restaurant. He bent down to see under the hats and hoods of those around him, conscious that he was startling them but not caring. In the end he found her in the cabin, her head in her hands. She told him she'd thrown up. She didn't like boats much in general, she reminded him, and looking at the falls had made her dizzy. "I didn't want you to miss them, though," she told him, and he could see she'd been crying. He put his arm around her, and they sat like that until the trip was over. The other passengers began to file into the cabin around them, taking off their hats and jackets and hanging them on pegs until only Henry and Helen were left in theirs.

They had planned to go on into Canada that afternoon, the first time they'd been out of the country since Korea, but instead they turned around, headed back the way they'd come. It was late afternoon, but Henry figured they could be home by midnight if he got a clear run and put his foot down.

•

The colonel has a few more questions, and he asks if they'd mind talking to him separately. Henry feels himself stiffen, but Helen says, "Of course." He can tell she wants to go first, so he gets up

and says he'll take a walk. He'll be back in about fifteen minutes.
He steps out into the hall and finds his topcoat and hat and calls
for Denny, Helen's dog. He walks out back first, and from the
yard he can see Helen inside with the colonel. He wonders what
she's saying as the dog strains at the leash. Probably talking more
about her dreams. She thinks maybe the little gray men took one
of her eggs. She thinks she remembers being shown strange children. They had agreed that she wouldn't talk about this, but
Henry realizes suddenly he doesn't trust her. It makes him shudder to think of her telling these things to a stranger.

When he takes Denny around the front of the house, he is
startled to find a black man in his drive, smoking. The young
man drops the cigarette quickly when Denny starts yapping. He
is in an air force uniform, and Henry realizes that this must be
the colonel's driver. He feels suddenly shy. He tells him, "You
startled me," and the young airman says, "Sorry, sir." And after a
moment, that seems all there is to say. That *sir*. Henry lets
Denny pull him up the drive, whining. The poor dog hasn't been
out for hours and as soon as they're at the end of the drive squats
and poops in full view of the house. Henry holds the leash slack
and looks the other way. When they walk back a few minutes
later, the airman is in the colonel's car. The windows are fogged.
Henry knocks on the driver's-side glass.

"Would you like a cup of coffee?"

The airman hesitates, but his breath, even in the car, is
steaming.

"I could bring it out," Henry offers, and the young man says,
"Thank you." And it's the lack of a *sir* that makes Henry happy.
He takes Denny inside and comes back out in a few minutes with
two cups of coffee and climbs into the car with the boy. He sets

them on the dash, where they make twin crescents of condensation on the windshield. When Henry sips his coffee, he realizes he's left his teeth inside with Helen, and he's suddenly self-conscious. He thinks he must look like an old fool, and he wants to be silent, keep his mouth shut, but it's too late. The airman asks him how he lost them.

"A fight," Henry says. And he tells a story he's never told Helen, how he got waylaid by a couple of crackers when he was just a boy. They wanted to know his mama's name, but for some reason he refused to say. "I just call her Mama," he said. "Other folks call her Mrs. Hull." But the boys wanted to know her first name, "her Chrustian name." Henry just kept on saying he didn't know it and then he tried to push past them and leave, but they shoved him back and lit into him. "I don't know what I was thinking," he says now over his coffee, "but it was very important to me that those fellas not know my mama's name. Mrs. Hull's all I'd say. I knew it, of course, although I never called her by it or even rightly thought of her by it. But I'd be damned if I'd tell them, and they beat the tar out of me for keeping that secret."

"Yeah, but I bet those boys got their share," the airman says, and Henry smiles and nods. He can't be more than eighteen, this driver. They talk about the service. The boy is frustrated to be a driver in the air force. He wants to fly. Henry tells him how he was put in the signals corps: "They liked having me fetch and carry the messages." The boy, Henry thinks, is a good soldier, and he feels a surge of pride in him. But then the coffee is finished and Helen is at the front door.

"Henry!" She doesn't see him in the car. "Henry!" He's suddenly embarrassed and gets out of the car quickly. "There you are," she says. "It's your turn."

Henry ducks his head back into the car to take the empty mugs and sees the airman looking at him strangely. "Eunice," he offers awkwardly. The young man's face is blank. "My mother's name. Eunice Euphonia Hull. In case you was wondering." He closes the car door with his rear, moves toward the house. Inside, he hands Helen the two mugs, and she takes them to wash up.

Back on the sofa, Henry sees that his dentures are lying beside the plate of sandwiches, but he feels uncomfortable about putting them in now.

The colonel asks him to describe his experiences, and Henry repeats the whole story. They'd been making good time until the cop stopped them around ten-thirty, and even then Henry had still expected to make it home by one. He explains how they noticed the lights a little after that and about twenty minutes later how they began to sense that the object was following them, how he had sped up, how it had kept pace. Finally he describes it swooping low over the road in front of them and hovering a hundred yards to their right. He'd stopped, still thinking it could be a chopper, and got out with the binoculars, leaving Helen in the still running car. But after getting a closer look he'd become uneasy, run back, and they had left in a hurry. They couldn't have been stopped more than ten minutes, but when they got home it was almost dawn, hours later than they expected.

"Mrs. Hull," the colonel says, "claims you were screaming when you came back to the car. About being captured."

Henry feels a moment of irritation at Helen.

"I was yelling," he says. "I was frightened. I felt that we were in danger, although I couldn't tell you why. I just knew this wasn't anything I understood."

He pauses, but the colonel seems to be waiting for him to go on.

"I was in Korea. I mean, I've been under fire. I was never afraid like this."

"These dreams of your wife's," the colonel asks. "Can you explain them at all?"

"She believes them," Henry says quickly. "Says they're more vivid than any dreams she remembers."

"Can you think of anything else that might explain them?"

Henry pauses. He could end it all here, he thinks. He looks at his dentures on the coffee table, feels the flush of humiliation. He opens his mouth, closes it, slowly shakes his head.

The colonel waits a moment, as if for something more. Then: "Any dreams yourself?"

"No, sir," Henry says quickly. "I don't remember my dreams."

The colonel clicks his pen—closed, open, closed—calls Helen back in, thanks them both for their time. He declines another sandwich, puts his cap under his arm, says he must be going, and they follow him out to where his driver holds the door for him. The car backs out, and they watch its taillights follow the curve of the road for a minute. Henry wonders if the colonel and his driver will talk. If the colonel will make fun of their story. The thought of the young man laughing at him makes him tired. But then he thinks, no, the colonel and the airman won't share a word. The boy will just drive, and in the back seat the colonel will watch him. Henry feels like he let the boy down, and is suddenly ashamed.

They stand under the porch light until the car is out of sight. "Well," Helen says, and he sees she's glowing, almost incandescent with excitement. "I think we did the right thing, don't you?" He feels his own mood like a shadow of hers. Bugs ping against the bulb and he flicks the switch off. In the darkness, they're silent for a moment, and then he hears the squeal of the screen door as she goes inside.

It's not late, but Helen tells him she's about done in. The interview went on for almost four hours. She goes up to bed, and Henry picks up in the living room, carries the cups and plates through to the kitchen, fills the sink to soak them. The untouched sandwiches he covers in Saran Wrap and slides into the refrigerator. He drops his dentures in a glass of water, watches them sink. Then he goes up and changes into his pajamas, lays himself down beside his already sleeping wife, listens to her steady breathing, dreams about the future.

A few weeks later they'll receive an official letter thanking them for their cooperation but offering no explanation for what they've seen. Henry hopes Helen will let the matter drop there, but she won't. She wants answers, and she feels it's their duty to share these experiences. "What if other people have had them?" They'll meet with psychiatrists. They'll undergo therapy. Henry shows symptoms of nervous anxiety, the doctors will say, but they won't know why. Eventually, almost a year later, under hypnosis, Henry will recall being inside the ship. He and Helen will listen to a tape of his flat voice describing his experiences. Tears will form in Helen's eyes.

"It's as if I'm asleep," he'll say on the tape. "Or sleepwalking. Like I'm drugged or under some mind control."

Under hypnosis, Henry will remember pale figures stopping their car. He'll recall the ship—a blinding wall of light—and being led to it, as if on an invisible rope, dragged and stumbling, his hands somehow tied behind him. He'll remember being naked, surrounded, the aliens touching him, pinching his arms and legs, peeling his lips back to examine his gritted teeth, cupping and prodding his genitals. It'll all come back to him: running through the woods, the breeze creaking in the branches, tripping and staring up at the moonlit trees. "Like great white sails," he'll hear himself say thickly as the spool runs out.

Afterward, he'll tell Helen in a rage he's finished with shrinks, but in the months that follow she'll call more doctors and scientists. She'll say she wants to write a book. Something extraordinary has happened to them. They've been chosen for a purpose. She'll talk to journalists. Henry will refuse to discuss it further. They'll fight, go days without speaking.

Tonight, in his dream, Henry wakes with a violent shudder, listens to his heart slow. He's lying in bed with Helen, he tells himself. He can feel her warm breath on his back. She rolls over beside him, the familiar shifting and settling weight, but then he feels the strange sensation of the mattress stiffening, the springs releasing. He opens his eyes and sees his wife rising above the bed, inch by inexorable inch, in a thin blue light.

BRAVE GIRL

FILLINGS WERE GOOD for groans. There was something about the contrast between the low, jumbled moans and the high-pitched whine of the drill, not quite drowning them out. Sometimes the mewling would sound almost like words, like Chewbacca in *Star Wars*, full of feeling but without meaning. It was impossible to form real words with the steel tang of my father's instruments on your tongue, his rubber-gloved knuckles pressing into the corners of your mouth.

Fillings were good. Sometimes there were even tears. But extractions were better. Extractions made kids scream.

My father would stand back a little after the first examination and say, "Rinse now," and then, when the patient was lying back in the chair, try to break the news gently. "I'm not going to hurt you," he'd tell them, and they'd pale. "You don't believe me, but you will. Promise. You want to know why?" He'd put his hand on his heart. "Because it's the *tooth*." That might even make them smile, but soon there'd be tears, and they'd just be the start. My father would say something about an injection, but even that wouldn't do it. Kids who'd never had an extraction thought that an injection meant a shot in the arm. The real moment was when he held up the silver syringe, with its glistening tip of Novocain shining wetly in the bright halogen lights. "Just a little pinch," my father would say. "Open wide." That was when the yelling would start, the needle bearing down on you, vanishing from sight into your mouth.

I was ten that summer, almost eleven, old enough to look after myself at home, but my father insisted on taking me with him to work. In the spring my mother had moved to London with her captain from the Territorial Army (he was a gynecologist in real life), and my father didn't like me being alone in the house. He'd demanded that I finish the term at my old school and spend half the summer with him, but now it was the second Friday in July, and on Sunday I would go away to live with my mother and Captain Cunt.

My mother had left me her white overnight case. It was round and silk-lined, and just the right size for me. It had a vanity mirror in the lid in which I loved to stare at myself. Soon I'd be packing it.

"I could fight her for custody, sweetheart," my father had told me. "And I'd probably lose. But I want you to know I love you, and if you want to stay, I'll do everything in my power. No ifs and buts about it. It's your choice; you just say the word."

I told him I knew he loved me. And I did. But I also knew I was the only one left for him to love, and when he said things like that it made me worry that I didn't love him enough. I didn't want to choose. I already felt sorry for him because my mother had left. I tried to make up for it by being good.

•

It wasn't so bad at the surgery. I even had my own room, a tiny cubicle intended for gas extractions but rarely used by my father, who referred most of that work to the hospital. There was still a high bed, upholstered in blistered red vinyl, and a tall stainless steel instrument tray which I could use as a desk. Every morning, before he opened, my father would let me into the waiting room to take my pick of the new comics and magazines. I would come back with yellowed dog-eared armfuls of *Mandy* and *Jackie* and the occasional copy of boys' comics like *Battle* or *Warlord*, the ink smelling like pee. Buried deep in the pile would be one or two slippery editions of *Cosmopolitan* or *Elle* that my father's Australian nurse, Sylvia, subscribed to and left in the waiting room for mothers. At the start of the summer I had read my way through most of the girls' comics and grown bored. The boys' comics with their tales of torture and heroism had entertained me briefly (I was especially struck by a strip called *Sergeant Steele*, about a self-sacrificing NCO with a bullet next to his heart — "like a time bomb in his chest!" — who stayed on at the front to perform weekly feats of suicidal bravery). But lately I was onto a steady diet of slick grown-up magazines. I would close the blinds on the window and skim through the pages to see how many stories there were about sex. I tried to memorize all the tips: seven secrets of office romance; nine lives of modern women; ten telltale signs he's interested. I couldn't imagine my parents doing any of the things the stories described, so I pictured blond Sylvia, in her short dental nurse's uniform and white tights, winning and keeping men, enjoying a career and multiple orgasms. Sylvia would be good at all that, I thought, and I admired her. If there were no new *Cosmo*s or *Elle*s, I'd settle for the duller articles in *Woman's Own* about family life.

The only thing that would tear me away from a good article about sex was moans or cries from the other room.

•

The girl in the chair on my last day at the surgery had been ice skating with friends. It was her birthday party. Most of them hadn't known how to skate, and they'd been circling the rink hanging on to the sides and making short staggering runs back and forth across the ice. On one of these, the birthday girl had dropped behind the others. They'd reached the barrier and slumped across it, and in her hurry to catch up she'd stumbled and slid on her stomach toward them. Someone had lost their balance, and the back of a skate had slipped out and caught the fallen girl in the face. Her two front teeth went *snap* like a pencil lead.

My father was pushing cotton wadding into her mouth, his fingers working quickly like a magician's, shoving in more and more of the short white swabs until her cheeks bulged like a hamster's. Then, just as fast, he was pulling them out one after another, limp with blood. He dropped them with his tweezers into the metal pan that Sylvia, his beautiful assistant, held out for him.

The girl was lying almost horizontal and raised up for my father to work on without straining his back. My head, when I took my usual position in front of the chair, was at her shoe level. It took a moment for her to see me standing there, staring, and her eyes grew huge around her tiny pupils.

I never said anything when I watched my father work. I never really showed any expression. I just wanted to let the kids know I was there. I liked to think I was helping him. Sometimes he told them how traveling dentists in olden days often drew a crowd. I was sure my presence could shame some of the kids into not going mental. It was a playground thing. What I held over them, like a knife at their throats, was my contempt.

"Hello, darling," my father said, but his glance at me was so fleeting his expression didn't change. He picked up his drill and thumbed it for a second to get the girl used to the sound. "Now, this will only tickle, sweetheart," he told her over the whir of the motor. He showed her the air-blower and the water jet and called them his toys. A little later, he held up a hypodermic and told her it would only sting a bit. He said these things so often that I thought he believed them. You couldn't see his lips move behind his mask, but if you looked closely you could see the paper crimp at his mouth.

My father talked to all his patients. He asked them their names and then he talked to them as though he'd known them all their lives. This girl's name was Marie. He told Marie how good she was. What a big girl Marie was being. He told her how proud her parents would be. He called her mother *mummy* and her father *daddy*. It was odd hearing him talk like that to a stranger. It reminded me of how he had sat down one evening and answered my questions about the divorce.

"The tooth?" he lisped, but I didn't smile. "Mummy and Daddy fell out of love." The way he said it made me think of falling out of treehouses, or swings, off bicycles or ponies — all the ways kids ended up in his surgery. "People change," he said. I told him I'd never change, but he said I was being silly. "Don't you want to grow up?" he asked me gently, and I shook my head till my temples ached and he caught me and held me.

I glared up at the girl. She was older than me — twelve, perhaps thirteen — and she had lipstick on, a dark cherry that seemed almost black against her pale skin. She wore tight designer jeans and a white blouse freckled with blood. I could see her bra through the polyester, and I watched her small chest heaving.

She was in too much pain and shock to scream, but she was

shuddering with sobs and whinnying nasally. I wanted to tell her to stop having an eppy. But my father spoke to her softly as he worked, while Sylvia stroked her forehead, her bright nails in the girl's fringe. The three of them reminded me of a funny sort of family. After a little while the girl's moans became weaker and fuzzier, and I knew the injection was taking effect. My father reached into her mouth with his shiny pliers and pulled the broken stubs of teeth out one at a time. He had long, strong fingers, only slightly hairy, and I saw them go white, straining. He held each tooth up, streaky with blood, and studied it for a second. He looked like a doctor in the westerns he loved who'd just extracted a bullet from deep in the hero's leg. Then he dropped the teeth into a kidney-shaped bowl, where they made a dull *ping* on the stainless steel.

"All done," he said cheerfully. "There's a brave girl."

She smiled at him numbly, her cherry lips opening over the dark gap in her teeth.

•

For as long as I could remember, I had been the bravest kid I knew. Everyone else was afraid of the dentist — even boys. My father's surgery was close to school, and most of my friends were his patients. I was sure they were scared of him. It made me secretly proud.

That summer, though, I had started to be afraid. I knew that my father would never let me go ice skating now. The year before he'd had a girl come in who'd lost several teeth playing hockey and he'd made me take netball at school. Last spring the police had used his records to identify the body of a boy who'd drowned and I'd had to give up piano and take swimming lessons instead. It had bothered me then, but now I knew that when he banned skating I would be glad. Even if my mother let me, I decided I didn't want to.

I was afraid of other things too. My friends had begun to get their ears pierced and I wanted to, but I was frightened. They all had their mothers to take them and give permission for the man to place the gun to their ears. I couldn't imagine my father there with me. Sharon Clark in my class had gone with her mother, and she said proudly it *hurt like hell*. That made me feel faint. I thought of buying bras. I thought of getting my period. I didn't want to leave my father, but I knew I'd go to my mother. I loved her too, of course, but next to fear, love just didn't seem like a useful way of choosing between your parents.

My mother called me almost every night, and because we couldn't talk about her and my father, we talked about the captain. I asked her what he did in the TA, and she said she wasn't sure. "Only he can't be a gynecologist," I said. I'd only learned the word recently. Guy-neck-ologist. I liked to say it. "There's not much call for gynecologists in the army. I mean, what would a gynecologist do at the front?" She laughed a little and told me she didn't know, but I had my suspicions. He was handsome, the captain, tall and fair. He looked like the Nazi interrogators in my comics. The kind of man who made people betray their comrades. Everyone cracked under torture, sooner or later, I knew.

Sometimes the captain would come on the line. I liked to call him sir. He thought I was very polite. He told me how much fun we'd all have together. "What do you like to do?" he asked, and I told him I liked going to work with my dad. "Could *we* do that, sir?" But the captain just coughed. "I mean when you're being a soldier," I said. "Not looking up people's *fannies*."

During the days I read *Cosmo* and tried to make friends with Sylvia. I told her I liked her nail polish, and she showed me how to put it on in long tapering strokes. She was younger and prettier than my mother, just like the captain was cleverer and richer than my father. I wanted to get her alone, to make her a confidante. I would tell her how nice my father was. I thought if he had her, I wouldn't feel so bad about leaving. Perhaps I could even stay. But I could never find the right moment. Sylvia insisted on treating me like a kid even though I knew all her sex tips.

"My dad likes nail polish," I said.

"Really?" She took my hand in hers. "Let's just see what we can do with these nails of yours, eh?"

"Don't you think he's good-looking?" I asked her coyly and she whispered back, "Fair dinkum. If he was my dad, I'd be really proud of him." I wasn't sure who was trying to convince whom.

In between patients, my father would slip the mask down around his neck and try to entertain me. Sometimes he would pull out a matchbox, empty the matches into a pocket, and drop a shiny globe of mercury into the little drawer. He would tip it back and forth under my nose. "See," he'd say. "A little mouse." And I'd go, "Oh yeah." I preferred it when Sylvia gave me the used drill bits to collect. They were diamond tipped and came in tiny plastic cubes the size of jewel boxes. "Your first sparklers," Sylvia whispered to me, and I told her that diamonds were a girl's best friend.

Once I heard my father tell her that she was good with me and that he appreciated it. "She has a bit of a crush on you," he said, which made me furious. After that I stopped trying to time my trips to the loo to coincide with hers.

•

The last patient that day was a boy called Barry, so scared he refused to sit still. His mother had to come in with him. As soon as she placed him in the chair and my father began raising it, he squirmed off. "I'll be good," he blubbed. "Honest." *What a spaz*, I thought. I would have liked to help, but when parents were in the surgery my father wanted me to keep out of the way. I satisfied myself with sitting in Sylvia's swivel chair, studying the chart on her clipboard, sucking her Bic.

"I promise this won't hurt," my father said soothingly, but the boy's mother was losing her patience.

"You'll just have to learn to put up with a little pain," she said, and I saw my father give her a sideways look. In the end he asked her to get into the chair with Barry in her lap. He tilted the chair back until mother and child were almost horizontal and then he raised the chair to work on the boy.

My father only worked on children. He preferred it that way. So when Barry pleaded, "Mummy first," and she said, "Oh, why not?" he paused for a moment. She had already closed her eyes and laid her head back in a pantomime of calm resignation. "Open wide?" Sylvia suggested, and my father began the examination. He was silent, though, as he probed the mother's teeth. He hadn't worked on adults for years, and he didn't know how to talk to them. When he bent over I could see that his bald spot, not much bigger than a ten-pence coin, was flushed. I hoped Sylvia wouldn't notice.

•

At five o'clock my father hung his white coat on the back of the door and looked suddenly smaller and older in his shirt and creased tie. "What a day," he said, dropping into the chair opposite Sylvia's desk. I was spinning around on an adjustable stool, holding my arms out and then bringing them in to my body and speeding up like a figure skater.

"You were a trouper with that Marie," Sylvia said, looking up from the chart she was completing.

"Thanks for your help with Barry and his mother," he replied, and she looked down as she passed the chart across to him. "Really," he said.

She got up and began collecting instruments from the trays.

"I'm lucky to have you, Sylvia," he said. I let my feet scuff the floor until my spinning came slowly to a rest. "You're the best nurse I've ever worked with."

"Well." She dropped the instruments into the sterilizer with a clank. "Cheers."

Her mask was lying on her desk where she had left it when she took it off to answer the phone. It was still bowed from her face, and leaning over, I could see in the center a smudge of lipstick. I slipped it over my mouth and smelled her perfume. I wondered if the lipstick would rub off on me. There was no makeup at home since my mother left.

"We make a good team, I think," my father went on. "The two of us."

He's paying her a compliment, I thought. It was a sign.

But Sylvia just shrugged her coat on. "Oh yeah." She laughed. "Torville and Dean. That's us, all right." She didn't look back at him, but at the door she stopped to blow me a kiss. "Be good, you. Ciao."

"See ya," I called through the mask, but my father just went back to his paperwork, pressing his signature firmly through the carbon paper.

•

Before he closed up, I made my father examine me. I could tell he was unhappy. After all the cowardly kids, the crybabies, I thought I could cheer him up by being the perfect patient.

"That Marie," I said scornfully, climbing into the chair. "They were her baby teeth, right?"

He shook his head. It seemed like a crime to lose your permanent teeth, and I was suddenly angry at the girl, although I also understood a little better why she had cried so much. My father had stickers that he gave out to his best patients: a bright, shining cartoon smile with the words "Teeth are for life."

I lay back while he pumped the pedal and felt myself floating up toward him. It was like being held in his arms, even better than the magic-carpet feeling of wafting down to earth later. He smiled at me over his mask—I could tell from the way his eyes went—and asked me to open wide, "wide as you can," and told me what a good girl I was, how brave I was. Just like he talked to any of the other kids. For once, I liked that. It was good to know he would love me even if I were a stranger.

He'd actually cried when they'd identified the body of the boy, his missing patient. I remembered it because it was the last time I'd seen my parents touch. We watched the announcement on the local news, and when I looked at my father the tears were dripping from his chin. He told us that the boy's father had called him that morning, wanting to know if there could be a mistake. "He asked me how I could be so sure when he couldn't even recognize his own son." My mother reached across and stroked the tears from his cheeks.

On that last afternoon at the surgery, I'd already made up my mind that if he found no work to do, I'd suggest he take an impression of my teeth. He'd fill two horseshoe-shaped troughs with pink goo, slip them into my mouth one at a time, and make me bite down hard. I liked leaving a perfect ring of toothmarks. The worst thing about it was that you felt as though your mouth were being stretched, as if you'd smiled too long, like Miss World. Afterward, he'd ask me if it was yummy — it was supposed to be strawberry flavored — but I'd tell him it tasted like a plastic spoon left in a bowl of fruit salad and make him laugh.

But that afternoon he found a slightly loose baby tooth and asked me if I wanted him to take it out or if I wanted just to let it work free. "It's up to you. But it'll mean an injection."

I swallowed my spit and told him to take it out anyway. I didn't know when he'd get another chance, and I didn't like the idea of another dentist doing it.

"Okay," he said. "If you're sure you're sure?"

I'd never had an injection before, but I watched coolly as he showed the needle to me and told me it would just pinch. "I *know*," I said. I watched it get closer until I couldn't keep it in focus any longer. Just for a second I thought about changing my mind, and then the needle was gone, out of sight, into my mouth.

Later, on the way home in the car, I couldn't stop touching my slack face. It felt different, I told my father — smoother, softer.

"Because you're feeling your face through your fingers. What's missing is the feel of your fingers *on* your face."

I turned that over for a long moment. "So this is how I feel to other people when they touch me?"

He nodded. I had been rubbing my face, trying to overcome the numbness, but now I stopped and touched myself, my lips, my chin, more gently.

It made me shiver. I blew my cheeks out and slapped them as hard as I could in time to the song on the radio. Then I folded down the vanity mirror and admired how rosy they were. I couldn't feel a thing. After the needle went in, I lost all sensation in my jaw, except at the last second I felt a sharp stabbing pain. For a moment, when it hurt, I thought something was wrong with me. I thought it was my fault. I was less brave than I should have been. And then it came to me: you couldn't be brave without being scared. Sergeant Steele knew it. "I'm no 'ero," he'd growl gruffly, turning down medals. "I've just got nuffin' to lose . . ."

But it also occurred to me in that moment of wincing pain that my father was a liar, that he lied every day of his life. And I was suddenly, enormously relieved.

•

At dinner he tried to say how much he'd miss me. I was drinking my milk through a straw and was distracted by the idea that the straw had a hole in it. When I realized it was lying in the new gap in my teeth, resting against the gum, I set the drink down quickly. "We'll still see each other on weekends and holidays," he was saying, and I nodded vigorously.

Afterward, I washed the tooth — an incisor, my father told me — under the kitchen tap and looked at it in my hand. It was funny to think it had been part of me. He asked me if I'd like to leave it under my pillow for the tooth fairy, but I told him I was too old for that, and he tried to smile. I didn't say, but I thought I'd show the tooth to my mother. I put it in a jam jar and shook it to hear the tiny sound of it beating on the glass. I decided to keep all my teeth.

But when my father came up to tuck me in, I told him I'd changed my mind. I gave him the tooth and told him I'd like to put it under my pillow. For a second it lay like a tiny bone in his hand, and then he folded it in his hankie and slid it under my head. He bent down to kiss me goodnight and then he was gone, pulling the door to within an inch of closing, the way I liked it. He smelled of tears.

I lay awake a long time after he left. In the bathroom, before bed, I had run my tongue, tangy with toothpaste, over the hole where the tooth had been, flicking the tip back and forth, not wanting to keep it there too long. There was something thrilling about the tingling feeling I got from that raw, tender spot. I looked at it in the mirror, and it looked very pink and shiny with saliva. I touched my finger to the gap, and it felt moist, slick. Now I lay there and thought of my new incisor pushing up into place, and I couldn't wait. I started checking the rest of my teeth, grabbing them one by one between two fingers, tugging, testing to see how firm they were.

THE NEXT LIFE

THE MOURNERS were playing poker around the rosewood table the night before his father's funeral, and Lim was winning.

They had begun the game to help themselves stay awake during the vigil. Pang had produced the new deck from a pocket of his white mourning suit and asked Lim's permission earlier in the evening. "It'll amuse the ghost," he said, indicating the casket. "Being able to see all our cards."

Now it was almost dawn, and Lim had been winning for an hour or more. It was uncomfortable. Where before they had talked softly among themselves, now they played in silence. Lim wished he could get up and leave, but it seemed improper to end the game ahead. Every time he told himself to fold he would look at his cards and find a pair of aces, a wild card, four cards to a flush — something too good to turn down. He bet heavily on mediocre hands, hoping to have his bluff called, but the others were afraid of his good fortune now. When one of them did stay in, Lim made a hand with his last card and still took the pot.

He fanned his cards to study them and thought of the coffin over his shoulder.

•

Lim had been determined to give his father the finest possible funeral. Old Lim had been the proprietor of the oldest Chinese newspaper on the West Coast. The day after his death of a second stroke, Lim had driven his prized Cadillac gingerly into Chinatown, to the corner of Jackson and Powell and the shop of Mr. Pang, the maker of grave goods.

The shop was on the second floor of a brick warehouse opposite the old Kong Chow Temple. At the top of the stairs a lighted glass cabinet was bright with spirit money, bricks of red-and-gold notes in neat, squat stacks. Beside them, through the narrow open door, Lim could see white paper furniture, and further back life-size paper suits hanging on the wall. He would need to buy all these items to burn at the funeral. Their smoke and ash would rise to heaven, where his father would be well provided for, as wealthy in the next life as in this.

Inside, he found Pang himself, seated at a long work table, fitting thin canes together to make the frame of a model house. Behind him a bundle of bamboo rested in a pan of boiling water, softening until it could be bent and shaped. Sheets of rice paper hung on wire racks above, fluttering gently in the breeze from the door. It was warm in the shop. Pang wore only shorts and an undershirt, and his shaved head above his half-moon glasses shone under the bright silver work lights. As Lim came forward, he stood and dried his hands on a rag, apologizing for the heat. "Air con dries the paper," he said, rubbing his thumb against his fingertips. "Makes it hard to work."

He led Lim into the back room of the shop, which doubled as a showroom and storage space. It was filled with paper houses and cars and, further back, whole rooms of ghost furniture. Everything was white, but the different items were made to mismatched scales. The furniture would not fit in the houses; the cars reached as high as the rooftops. There was something toy-like about the items on display, which reminded Lim of child-hood, and yet he walked among them like a giant. *So this*, he thought, *is what the afterlife looks like.*

With Pang's help he chose the best house in stock, with a bal-cony and a veranda, and an almost life-size paper sedan with the three-pointed Mercedes star fashioned in straw on its hood. Pang nodded his approval and went to the stairs and called his assistant to come and move the pieces to the back of the shop. A door opened, the sound of a television — the stuttered blows and grunts of a martial arts movie — floated down to them, and a stocky, muscular young man appeared. Pang gestured to him impatiently, pointing out with his chin the pieces Lim had chosen and whistling angrily when the youth stooped over the wrong one. Lim watched as he lifted the house and then the car high overhead and carried them away. At the door a breeze filled the paper shells with a snap, and the boy had to steady him-self to steer them through the opening while Pang hissed with displeasure.

They moved on to the furniture and Lim chose the best tables and chairs, even a paper TV and VCR. By the time Pang left him to write up the order, he had bought up almost half the stock. Alone in the showroom, Lim paced back and forth between the houses of the dead. Over the rooftops he saw the youth — a young man really, he decided — lighting a cigarette. He held the match in his hand, watched it burn down slowly till the yellow flame touched his fingertips, let it fall. When he noticed Lim watching, he stared back blankly, pantomimed the offer of a cigarette, but Lim shook his head. He heard Pang's footsteps re-turning and went to meet him.

"You make all the pieces yourself?" he asked, looking down

the list the old man presented to him. "Or does your assistant build some?"

"They're all my own work," Pang told him. "My son runs the press. To print the hell notes." Lim had bought several million dollars in the best gold-leaf spirit money.

He complimented the workmanship while Pang calculated the bill on an abacus. In the whiteness of the shop, the dark beads clacked back and forth. There was something soothing to Lim about the transaction and the other man's quiet business manner. "Isn't it hard to see your work burn?" he asked, and Pang nodded without looking up. He checked his figures twice and then named a price. It was a large sum, but Lim reached for his wallet and counted the bills out, one by one, with no word of bargaining. Pang blinked as each note was laid down, then shuffled them into a neat pile and put them in his pocket.

"My condolences," he said. "Your father was a great man."

Lim gave instructions for delivery to the cemetery and thanked him for his time. He made to leave, but paused and turned back. "Tell me," he said, "do you know where I might hire professional mourners?"

Pang looked doubtful. "It is the old custom."

Lim watched him tip the abacus slightly, the beads sliding silently to one side, erasing the last calculation.

"I would be very grateful . . ." he began.

"My own family, in fact, were once mourners," Pang said slowly. "I could perhaps find some to attend you."

Lim thanked him for his kindness.

•

The day before the funeral, with the casket lying behind screens in the house on Diamond Hill, friends and family members came to pay their respects. The casket was closed, but Lim's mother placed a gold-framed photograph of the deceased on the lid. It was an old studio pose of an intense young man in a dark suit and narrow tie, his hair shining like a movie star's. The photograph had been taken before Lim was born, and he hardly recognized his father. He complained to his mother, "He looks like a stranger."

"Such talk!" she cried. "How can he be a stranger? He looks like you in this picture."

Mr. Pang arrived early with three others. Two were old men, one a retired grocer, the other a former butcher, cousins of Pang's. The third was his brawny son. The son helped move the deceased's favorite chair beside the casket, while the old men laid out a table with Old Lim's glasses, Luckies, his preferred brand of cigarettes, and a bottle of Corvoisier. Pang poured a glass of brandy, lit a cigarette, and set it in a jade ashtray for the spirit to enjoy. Lim showed them where the bottles of liquor and the cartons of cigarettes his father used to bring back from his business trips to Taiwan were kept. "Duty-free," he told Pang's son, who whistled softly when he saw the hoard. The mourners would ensure that fresh cigarettes were lit every half-hour or so.

Dishes of Old Lim's favorite foods had already been prepared by the cook, and these were brought out now and set beside the coffin. The ginger bass, Lim saw, was a fish his father had caught himself and frozen. Fishing had become the old man's passion at the end of his life. Lim remembered one afternoon off Duxbury Reef. They were out for striped bass, but his father could reel in nothing but rockfish. He kept throwing one back and hooking another. The weather had begun to worsen and the fog to roll in, but he refused to turn back without a bass. And all the time he kept hooking rockfish. Finally, in frustration, he had started to use his pocket knife to blind the fish, gouging their eyes before tossing them, still thrashing, back into the water. "Teach them to take my bait." Lim had turned away but said nothing. He hung over the side, staring into the dark water, and feigned seasickness all the way in. Even as a grown man, he found, he was afraid of his father.

Pang sniffed appreciatively over the dish. "The spirit will smell the delicious aroma and come closer." Lim thought of the blind fish swimming in the darkness.

As the first guests came up the drive, Pang's son began to wail and the older men bent their heads. When they looked up, they had tears in their eyes. Lim was impressed. He had begun to worry about the expense of hiring mourners, but now, as he went to greet his visitors, he felt a deep satisfaction. These men would help the family shoulder the burden of grief. He was gratified when his father's business partners and his older relatives complimented him on finding such skillful mourners. He noticed a change in the way these people treated him. Some of the journalists and editors were his own age, but previously, at his father's office or the golf club, they had merely nodded to him or smiled politely while they addressed his father. Now they caught his eye and drew him aside to express their sympathy. His father had been a giant. He was a dutiful son. They were sure the newspaper would prosper. They had always known how proud his father was of him. Lim nodded. The old man had made a point of taking his partners past his son's desk, testing him on figures or summoning him with a snap of his fingers to bring new copy to his office while they sat and sipped tea. His father liked to boast about Lim's education — Berkeley, his M.B.A. — but also to joke about what they didn't teach you in college: greed, luck, how to cut throats. Lim supposed he had resented it, but abstractly. Whatever he felt toward his father had always come second to what his father thought of him.

Every so often Lim excused himself to see that the flow of refreshments from the kitchen was running smoothly. The faces of Mr. Pang and the older mourners, he noticed, were still wet with tears. He could not imagine how the dried-up old men could cry so long. Pang's son did not cry, but he was still wailing lustily, and Lim thought it had been a wise choice on Pang's part to bring a young man with such strong lungs. Some of his guests had told him that the wailing could be heard from the street. Even his mother, who had been concerned about the cost, was moved. She had scolded him that his father, who had always been careful with money, would not have appreciated such excess. But she took one look at the mourners and her own tears began to flow so swiftly she was surprised and tried to cup them in her hands.

•

In the evening, as the last guests departed, there was a small commotion. The wails of Pang's son suddenly ceased, and at the door, saying goodbye, Lim and his guests fell silent for a moment. When he had seen them off, he came back into the house and Pang's son approached him with a carton of cigarettes, almost crushed, gripped in his hand.

He held them out to Lim without a word.

"He means to apologize," Pang said in a pinched voice. "He was taking these."

Lim took the small box and stared at it dumbly. It felt so light in his hands. The young man stood before him, his head bowed, shoulders raised, hands behind his back, as if expecting a blow. Pang was waiting for him, he knew, but in his confusion Lim could only thank the youth.

"It's nothing," Lim said. "It's not important." He almost pressed the box back into the young man's hands, but he could see the flush on Pang's face and bald head, and he could not meet his eyes. He felt as if the old man was angry with him, but he did not know what to say, and he excused himself to lead his mother to bed.

She leaned heavily on the arm he offered her. "If you had done anything like that, your father would have whipped you," she whispered on the stairs. Lim nodded. He wondered if he had done the right thing, but he was glad he had stayed calm. He didn't want to be angry at the funeral. It would be unseemly.

At her door, his mother turned. "You have honored Bar-Bar today," she said. "He was always such a superstitious man. You remember? When you were a small boy, he used to call you names. Little pig. Ugly dog. He made you cry." She smiled ruefully. "You didn't understand. He was so proud of you. He thought if he praised you, demons would know how valuable you were and take you."

"I know," Lim told her. "I do understand. It's the custom."

"All this," she said, squeezing his hand. "I never knew you loved him so much."

Afterward, he stood at the door to his own room, turning the idea over in his mind like a bright coin. Perhaps he had loved his father, he told himself. Next to respect and obedience, love had always been an extravagance in their relationship. But the more he thought it, the more he believed it, until it seemed to him a sharp point of truth.

He stared at his bed, but for the first time that day he felt re-
laxed, not tired. He decided to go down again to where the
mourners were sitting up beside the casket to keep the spirit
company.

Lim found them playing cards. Earlier he had wondered
briefly if it was proper, but he trusted Pang not to suggest any
impropriety. He was a professional, after all. He had even asked
for their fee in advance so they could divide it up and have something to gamble with. Now he formally complimented Lim on
the success of the day and, after a moment of awkwardness, invited him to join them and make a fifth.

"I haven't played since I was a student," Lim told them, but he
pulled up a stool and Pang dealt him in. He had thought himself
a skillful player in college, betting quarters, but he felt out of
his depth with stakes of ten or twenty dollars. He watched the
other players carefully, but they betrayed little. Pang's son never
looked up from his cards, and the faces of the older mourners
were perfectly still, resting. Lim lost hand after hand.

"Your luck is lousy," Pang told him, less with sympathy than
with approval. "Only natural."

Lim played on, but his concentration was poor. He was rest-
less, thinking about reopening his father's office, the huge rolls
of white paper waiting for ink. He didn't mind that he was losing. He had taken a kind of pride in spending money on the funeral arrangements. The mourners had done a good job, and he
told himself he would think of his losses as a tip, but after a while
he grew bored. He had such bad cards the game held no interest. He folded again and got up to stretch his legs.

The others played on — Pang was betting hard and winning,
mostly at his son's expense — while Lim walked slowly over to

his father's casket. He ran his finger along the rich teak and sat for a moment in the chair, listening to the bets being called from the table. The ginger fish was cold and congealed. He picked up his father's spectacles from the table beside him and slipped them over his own ears as he had as a child. He blinked, dizzied by the blurred images through the thick glass. Over the lenses, he saw that the cigarette in its jade ashtray was out, and he tapped another from the pack and put it between his lips and lit it. His father had smoked to the end, but Lim had not had a cigarette for years. He took the smoke into his lungs and held it for a long moment before exhaling. He rested the cigarette on the ashtray. The smell reminded him of his father. He watched the smoke swim upward and thought of Old Lim inhaling in heaven. He picked up the glass and watched the brandy cling to its sides as he swirled it around. The rich sweet smell filled his nostrils as he held it close to his nose. He took a deep breath, as if for a dive, and before he knew it he'd put the glass to his lips. He held the brandy in his mouth for a second and swallowed. It was good. He set the glass down and refilled it carefully from the bottle and went back to the game.

They were playing five-card draw now, and Lim threw in his ante. His cards were poor, but out of decency he stayed in, made a flush on his last card, and won his first hand of the night. The others seemed surprised. They looked at the cards he had laid down, and he waited a moment before pulling the pot toward him.

"Luck," he said, shrugging.

After that he began to play with more care and found himself drawing better cards. He played out a few more hands and won two or three in a row. The pile of notes in front of him began to grow. He felt pleased, but a little embarrassed. These men were gambling with money he had paid them, and he was taking it back. The grocer and the butcher looked away now when he won and would not meet his eyes. After a while he noticed the silence, and to break it he asked the mourners about their work.

"It must be hard," he said. "Mourning for someone you never knew."

"My father taught me a little," Pang said. "When I was young he never let me cry. He used to threaten me with a cane. When a pet died or when a toy broke, he told me to laugh. That way mourners saved up their tears for when they needed them."

"And does it work?" Lim asked. He found it hard to imagine Pang as a child with a father. He took two cards. He was working, skeptically, on a low straight, thinking if he made it he would win; if he didn't, he could give back some of the money he'd taken.

"For me," Pang said. He drew one card. "I've known others taught to wail and scream as children to build their strength." He shrugged, and Lim decided, almost with relief, that he had made a flush or a full house. "Your bet."

Lim threw in money and the bet was seen until it came round to Pang, who raised it with a small flourish. The light glinted off his glasses as he dipped his head to study his hand. His son looked at the crumpled notes still in front of him — he had lost almost all his earnings from the mourning — and scattered them over the center of the table. But at the next raise, he folded out of turn.

Pang gave a little snort and laid down a fifty.

Lim saw the bet and after a moment raised. What did it matter? he thought. His father was dead. Losing was nothing. He welcomed it. Dawn was breaking over the curving palms, and the gulls, clustered on the telephone lines, were waking.

The bet revolved until Pang raised it once more. He looked around the table confidently and the old men folded wearily, one after the other, until only Lim remained. He could have called—should have—but instead he raised again. Pang studied him closely, and Lim looked back at the cards fanned in his hand, suddenly ashamed of his recklessness, embarrassed by his play.

"You're wasting your money, I think," Pang said. He raised again.

Lim looked at his cards, looked at the pile of notes by his elbow, but all he could think of was the trace of emphasis Pang had placed on the word *your.* He felt something pressing him on, and he slid the cash into the center of the table. He regretted it immediately, hunched his shoulders and covered his cards, but when he glanced up he caught a look of fear on Pang's face and felt a kind of thrill.

Pang gathered together his own stack of remaining notes, counted them slowly from one hand to the other, straightened them into a neat bundle.

"Call," he said at length. "With this"—he pushed the money forward—"and I refund you for the grave goods, yes?"

Lim stared at him, and Pang nodded fiercely.

"The funeral," he whispered. "For free."

Lim rested his cards on edge against the table for a second, tapped them once, finally let them fall open. He'd made his low straight, but the cards in their whiteness seemed so insubstantial to him. He stared at a small crease across the corner of one of them. *Just paper after all,* he thought. There must have been nine hundred dollars on the table. Lim shuddered a little in the morning chill.

Opposite him, Pang's son sat very still. But Pang himself just shook his head and started to laugh. "Take it," he said, smiling crookedly at the money. "Take it. It's yours."

Lim looked at him and began to smile too. He saw the flicker of distaste on the faces of the older mourners, but that too seemed funny. He was still smiling as he drew the money into his arms, like an embrace.

•

The funeral took place in the old Chinese cemetery at Colma. Lim dimly recalled a festival day years earlier: white ash like snow, rising from every part of the dark graveyard. Now he watched the paper Mercedes burn. He stared into the leaping, dancing fire, letting the heat wash over him until he felt his eyes begin to smart and finally prick with tears. Pang had told him that it took almost thirty hours to build such a car, the house another twenty, and each piece of paper furniture at least three or four. Lim saw the flames eat them, lighting them like festive lanterns before stripping the paper from the bamboo skeletons. He stepped forward to lay one of the empty paper suits on the smoldering coals, but it fluttered in the smoke and he had to hold it until it flared. He felt the hairs on his knuckles shrink and pull tight. The heat caused an updraft, and the smoke and ashes ascended almost vertically. With them went the wails of the mourners, their voices cracking in the parched air, and Lim marveled with a new appreciation at their art.

He caught Pang's eye, and as the older man paused to fill his lungs, Lim bent and threw another bundle of spirit money into the brazier at the foot of the grave. He watched as the notes turned white and scattered in the wind of the flames. The scorched breeze flickered over him, plucking at his sleeve, his lapel, as if it might swirl him away with the ashes falling softly into the sky above. And for a moment he felt himself rise up with them — light as paper, buoyant with heat — until the cries of the mourners sounded only faintly below him.

SMALL WORLD

IS IT CHEATING? Wilson asks himself, watching her sprinkle salt on the bridge of skin between her thumb and index finger. Is it cheating to sleep with an ex-girlfriend? The question forms slowly, hangs there. He's been drinking all night. *They've* been drinking all night. First the grown-up drinks: martinis before dinner, a nice merlot with, a cognac after. And now, at the bar, shots. Against the cold, she says, nodding at the snow falling past the neon lattice of a Guinness sign in the window. For old times' sake.

He takes the salt shaker from her and makes a small pile of crystals on his own hand. Stray grains bounce and scatter on the bar. She lowers her head, glances up at him from under her brows, and he dips his own face, reaches out his tongue, draws it through the salt.

He is aware of her head tipping back beside him as he throws his own shot down.

Well, is it? he asks himself, eyes watering. With an ex?

He supposes so. Technically. But surely, the casuist inside him, the Jesuit schoolboy, wonders, surely there's some dispensation. After all, it's not someone new. It's someone old. Someone who pre-dates your wife. Someone you've cheated on already (so you owe her) or who's cheated on you (so you're owed). Not cheated on in the conventional sense, maybe, while you were still together, a couple, an *item*, but cheated on in a primordial sense. That moment of guilt, of memory, of *comparison* between the last fuck and the latest.

He bites down on the lime.

That moment.

He blinks the tears from his eyes, and sees she is laughing at him.

"You used to be a better drinker," she says. There's a rime of salt on her lower lip, and in reflex he licks his own.

"Out of practice," he tells her, but not why. Apart from rare nights sitting up alone in front of the tube with a glass of Bushmills, he's sworn off, to make it easier for his wife to go without during her pregnancy.

"A regular churchgoer," she teases, but he shakes his head. "You infidel."

•

In the Back Bay everything has changed. The Big Dig seems to have buried everything Wilson remembers. On Atlantic he doesn't recognize any of the stores. Near Fenway a bar he thought he recalled going to with his father is a sub shop. He's in actuarial research, an underwriter of new risks — next-generation chips, satellites, freak weather patterns — attending a conference on risk assessment at BU. When he tries to take two Berkeley mathematicians to dinner, nothing is where it's supposed to be. "I thought you grew up here," one of them says, laughing, and he tells him sharply, "Somerville. Not Boston." Finally, freezing, they go to the Pru, to the Top of the Hub, like any fucking tourists. And so he sits there, surrounded by the conference crowd, looking down on the city he grew up in. He can see the John Hancock building, the light on top red for snow. He can see the Citgo sign. He can see the river. He looks down on his childhood from behind double glazing.

Later, at the hotel, he calls his wife. He wants the reassurance of talking to someone who knows him. But she's not home yet. It's eight o'clock in California. She's in patent law, and he remembers she planned to work late while he was away. He calls her office, but she's not there either. In transit, then.

Bored, he glances at the price list for the minibar, flicks through the phone book. On a whim he looks for his own name. There it is, a string of them, like a list of descendants, but none of the initials are his, or his father's. The last memory he has of Somerville is the family kitchen, in '76. He'd known it was coming, and he was ready for them with his anger. His mother told him the divorce wouldn't change the way they felt about him: "We both still love you just the same." His father nodded, but Wilson said he didn't believe it. "You used to say you loved each other," he sneered. She tried to explain that it was different, what they felt for him and what they felt for each other, but he told her, "It's love, isn't it? It's all love." And something about the way he said it, how he looked at her, the bitterness, the anger, as if it were her fault that she was being cheated on, reduced her to tears for the first time in the whole sorry business. She jerked back from the table and went up to her bedroom—hers alone now—not wanting his father to see her tears. And they'd been left alone, he and his old man, who hadn't been home for a week, who was only there now for this last family meeting.

"Now look what you've done," his father said, and Wilson laughed bitterly. Slowly, ruefully, his dad smiled too, recognizing that he'd lost the power to make his son feel guilty. Because Wilson didn't feel guilty—not then, at least, although later guilt would be almost all he felt—just frustrated. It wasn't that he thought his mother was lying. He didn't distrust her, or even his father, when they said they loved him. He simply didn't trust their capacity for love, which was even worse.

"What can I say?" his father asked, but Wilson just looked away. His father got up, poured himself a shot, said, "Listen," and told Wilson about his birth. How Wilson had been a pree-mie, how the doctors had put him in the ICN, in an incubator, and his parents had watched him through a plate glass window, his mother from a wheelchair. "You were a marvel," his father said. "So small. So pink. Curled up, with your tiny fists to your chest."

"Spare me," Wilson said, but his father pushed on.

"We loved you that much. We both felt it—we expected it, of course, but it still surprised us, hey, how intense it was."

He stopped for a moment and glanced at Wilson, who said flatly, "So what?"

"So," his father replied a little roughly, "so afterwards, after we brought you home and we got to thinking about how much we loved you, we realized that what we'd felt before, what we thought was love, for each other, it wasn't the same thing."

He paused, and Wilson looked over and saw that he was staring at him.

"Does that explain it any better?"

And Wilson nodded, unable to speak, because it did; he did understand. He understood that his parents loved him and he understood that he'd driven them apart.

He tries his wife again, punching in the calling-card numbers deliberately, but hangs up before the machine cuts in. In the phone book, he looks for old friends. Dick Keane. Ryan Lynch. No listings. Dan Murphy could be any one of a dozen D. Murphys. The thought of calling them all makes Wilson feel tired. Dan, he thinks. Got Angela Quinn, the redhead, pregnant at sixteen, married her, dropped out. He looks for a listing of D. and A. Murphy. Nothing. Even the high school dropouts are gone. And because he has given up hope, he looks idly, flicking through the pages, just trying to remember names and faces. That's how he finds Joyce's name. J. Limerick. It has to be her. Joyce, he thinks. Still going by her own name. Limerick. He writes the number down, the hotel pen on the hotel pad. He'll never use it, after all. After all these years. He remembers getting her old number, the first time. The piece of paper he kept it on, soft and fuzzy from being folded and unfolded, tucked in a wallet for years, long after he'd moved away, long after he could have still called her.

And in the middle of it all the phone rings, as if he's willed it, and he jumps because he doesn't believe in such things.

"Hello?" he says.

"Hello yourself," his wife says.

She asks him what he's doing and he tells her, "Nothing. Debating whether to break into my minibar."

"Too sad," she says. "You don't want to be drinking alone."

"Vodka, Scotch, tiny tequilas. That's pretty good company. A whole miniature world of booze."

"Not to mention those ten-dollar macadamias," she says. "Whoever invented those things must have made a killing."

"Unless the legend is true and they were once free," he tells her. "Now all that's left is the vestigial free mint on the pillow."

She laughs with relief. They've fought. She didn't want him to take this trip. So now she says she loves him. "We miss you." And it takes him a moment to understand she means herself and the baby. She asks him to hold on a second, and the line goes quiet. He wonders where she's gone, and then she's back. "Could you hear her?" And he realizes she's been holding the phone to her belly. "Say something," she tells him, and the line goes quiet again. "Like what?" he asks. "Hello?" And then he falls silent, listening. He imagines her lying back on the sofa, dress unbuttoned, pressing the receiver to her stomach, round as a globe. It reminds him of the nurse running the ultrasound wand over her gooseflesh, the sonar pulse of the baby's heart and the grainy pixelated image he keeps in his wallet of the tucked, clenched form, a smudged question mark curled inside her. All he can hear now, very faintly, is the sea, waves, like in a shell. He thinks it's the rubbing of the plastic on his wife's belly, the tiny slap and suck of her skin.

Afterward he sits in bed, chewing his chocolate mint, reading *What to Expect When You're Expecting*. The compressor of the minibar cuts out with a shiver of glass.

His wife is in her third trimester, and they haven't had sex in a long time. At first he was too protective of her, then she was too sick in the mornings, now she's just too big. It's uncomfortable, impossible. When he's in the mood, she fears for the baby. When he's not, she says he doesn't find her attractive anymore. He tells her she's paranoid; she tells him he missed his chance.

Instead, he's taken to masturbating, for the first time in years, in the shower or when she goes out for groceries. The A&P has never sounded so sexy to him. It makes him feel furtive, caught halfway between infidelity and adolescence, by turns ashamed and angry. Tonight, still on West Coast time, he can't sleep, touches himself, stops. He realizes with dismay that he misses the risk of being caught, wants her to catch him. At least, he tells himself, he doesn't do it to images of her. But when he finally sleeps he dreams of sex with her on top, her hard, heavy belly held over him, pinning him down, forcing the air from his chest, and when he wakes it is on the verge of a wet dream. He stumbles into the arctic whiteness of the bathroom, squinting against the fluorescent glare of his own reflection. In the morning, before he leaves, he puts the piece of hotel notepaper with the phone number in his pocket.

He carries it around all day at the conference. At lunch he tells the mathematicians from the night before, trying to sound casual but trying to prove he's *from* here, and regrets it at once. They give him shit, and it's like being back in high school. For dinner they want to go to the Bull and Finch and he blows them off, thinking, *Geeks!* Instead, he drives his rental car along the river: Storrow to the Longfellow Bridge with its salt-and-pepper pots, Mem. Drive, Mass. Ave to Central, Harvard Square, and finally to Johnny D's in Davis Square. After he parks he just walks for a while, slipping in the snow, until it feels like the roads are the same, the sidewalks, the gradients. He sees the streets of chainlink fences. He see the statues of the Virgin in every third yard. Mary on the half-shell, he remembers, grinning. Slummerville. It's coming back. He returns to the bar. Orders a beer. Asks for the phone.

She must think he's one of those telesales people, but then he says his name and there's a pause and her voice changes. "What a coincidence," she says; she just moved back to town six months ago. Afterward, waiting for her, he mouths the words to himself: What a coincidence. Small world. What's that line? he asks himself. In a big enough universe, anything can happen. And in a small enough world, he thinks. Something about the odds of it, he decides, the odds of his being here, of her still being in town, of its really being her, makes it feel implacably innocent — not like a choice, more like an accident of fate.

•

She teaches at the high school now, Joyce. "Substitute," she says, "but they say it'll be permanent in the spring." Her husband's a consultant for an educational software firm. He visits schools and colleges all over the country to give presentations. "This week St. Louis, I think." Wilson says he's in insurance but doesn't want her to think he's a claims adjuster.

"I was never very good with numbers," she reminds him, but he tries to tell her that what he does isn't traditional insurance: writing policies for cars, houses, even lives is just accounting, but with new ventures there aren't any statistics. "Risk assessment isn't even about numbers, really," he says. "It doesn't matter if the chance of a car wreck is a million times higher than the probability of a radiation leak. People want to take their own risks, not have others impose them. Plus it's not the size of the risk that counts, it's the size of the consequences. The chance of getting caught might be vanishing, but if the penalty is bad enough, it changes the equation."

She tells him, "It all sounds very Catholic," and he lets it drop.

They make light, competitive small talk over dinner. Who remembers what. SAT scores. Colleges. Catching up with each other. Her honeymoon was on St. Barts. His handicap is fifteen. Her husband's is twelve. "One to me," she laughs, licking her finger and drawing a line in the air. She has three kids — three! — she says; six, five, and two; boy, girl, boy. "Wow," he responds.

"You wouldn't be so wowed if you had any yourself, I'm thinking?" she says, and he smiles and looks in his drink and slowly shakes his head.

"Okay, okay," he says. "You win. Game over."

She tells him she'll drink to that, and after a moment she asks after his parents and he after hers, and it doesn't seem odd to him that these are their common points of reference.

He dated her while his parents' marriage fell apart. Back then, in their Irish Catholic enclave (not quite a neighborhood, but a kind of satellite, a moon of Southie, the main Irish community), he was the first kid he knew whose parents were divorcing. It made him feel watched, the worst thing for a fifteen-year-old. He felt as if he were on a cliff, on the edge of something, feeling that pressure at the back of his knees to jump before he fell. So he broke a few windows, got in some fights, drank. Tried to cut a tragic figure by wearing black and listening to the Clash. And people — kids, their parents — shook their heads but let him get away with it, made allowances. Joyce was the only one who wouldn't tolerate him. She was in all honors classes, he in math only. When he made fun of her last name — "There once was a girl from Nantucket" — she came right back: "Who told some chickenshit to shut it." He called her *cunt* and she told him, "Using your parents as an excuse *is* chickenshit." Everyone else's gentle sympathy made him want to smash things; her frankness just made him want to talk. So he told her about his parents. And she was by turns curious, sad, outraged in ways that magnified his feelings. He told her he loved her, and it was such a relief to have someone to say it to. He even nursed a fantasy that his love for her could somehow inspire his parents. He touched her constantly in front of them, even though it made her squirm with embarrassment. Always an arm around her, holding hands, thigh to thigh. But his parents ignored them or, worse, seemed goaded to fight in front of her, until she insisted he spend more time at her place.

Joyce's parents, Mike and Moira, must have known about his home life, but they never talked about it, not a word, just welcomed him, treated him as if his being there every evening and all weekend were entirely normal. He became a fixture, ate with them, watched TV, took his turn washing up when Moira handed him a dishtowel, even went to church with them. Mike had been wary of Wilson at first, his reputation as a bad kid. Early on he'd taken him down to the basement, shown him his shotgun, his rifle, as if to say, *You're not so tough*. But Wilson's eyes had just lit up at the sight of the guns, their oily sheen. Besides, he knew Mike liked him. Joyce was the eldest of three girls, and Wilson figured her father enjoyed having a boy around (if only because he preferred to think of Wilson as a brother rather than a boyfriend to Joyce). It made him feel the value of being a son again, even as he felt guilty for cheating on his own parents.

One weekend when Joyce was down with the flu, Wilson looked so lost that Mike even invited him hunting. "Really?" "Sure," Mike said, although he had Moira call Wilson's mother for permission. "Hunting in New Hampster?" Joyce croaked, when Wilson was allowed to see her. "I know you don't want to turn into your dad. Just don't go turning into mine."

It was Wilson's first time, but he didn't admit it until Mike had parked the station wagon and they'd waded out into the snowy woods, for fear the trip would be canceled. Mike stopped in his tracks. "Your dad never took you?" he said, and then fell silent, embarrassed to have mentioned the unmentionable and for seeming to criticize. Wilson told him it was okay, but Mike was subdued all morning. At lunch he tried clumsily to apologize: "I could kick myself." Wilson, in trying to make him feel better, found himself talking about his parents. And once he began, unable to stop. Something about the woods, the cold, the guns beside them, the crouched anticipation of a deer, made him voluble. He even told Mike a dream he'd had of flicking through an old family photo album from back to front, seeing himself and his parents as they were now and then, as the pages turned, getting younger and younger. His father's hairline, his mother's hemline. Wilson himself playing with lost, broken toys, miraculously found and restored. Dropping to all fours, crawling, finally lifted up into their arms. "And in each photo they look happier and happier until in the very last, at the front of the book, they look as happy as I've ever seen them. And I'm gone."

He looked up and saw Mike staring at his hands, rotating the wedding ring on his finger. Wilson thought he was boring him, but then he saw him blinking, wiping his eyes. "The cold," Mike said when he saw Wilson staring, and Wilson looked away. He heard Mike pop a beer and in a moment felt the can being tapped against his arm.

"It's a mess, all right," Mike said, watching him drink. "But your folks, I'm sure they love you." And because it sounded like sympathy, because it sounded like a line of his parents', because he didn't want Mike to feel bad for him, Wilson said, "Fuck 'em." He meant it to be light, joky, a daring thing to say in front of an adult. But it didn't come out right. The coldness of the beer made him sound choked. There was a long pause, and then, as if in return, Mike told him how he'd met Moira, both of them in high school. "Married at seventeen, parents at eighteen." He shook his head. "We had no idea," he said. And Wilson nodded, overcome by this confidence and something more. Because wasn't that like him and Joyce? he thought. Wasn't that them? In high school. In love. "You understand, don't you?" her father was saying. And Wilson thought he did.

The week after, drunk on stolen whiskey, in bed with Joyce for the first time — Mike, Moira, and the girls out at the mall — they held each other, almost but not quite slept together. It was wonderful, clinging together on the brink of sex, and yet they never came as close again. A week later she told him it was over. And though he called and called, her phone just rang until Mike picked it up and stiffly told him not to call again. "Sorry, son," he said, while Wilson pleaded and cursed. "Sorry." A month later, Wilson and his mother were gone, first to his grandparents and then west.

So he and Joyce, over dinner and drinks, talk about their parents and not themselves.

Wilson's mother is remarried, he tells her, living in Lauderdale. His father is on Long Island with the latest in a string of girlfriends: the secretary he left Wilson's mother for; a waitress; now a nurse. "There are three things in every man's life he can be sure of," Wilson tells her in his father's voice. "Death, taxes, and a nurse." He shakes his head. "The nurse was his date at our wedding," he says. The funny thing, he tells her now, is that when he saw the wedding cake with its plastic bride and groom, he could think only of his parents, of their old wedding photo on the sideboard. He is silent a moment. After a second he asks about her folks, and she suggests the shots.

Her parents, she tells him at the bar, the drinks lined up before them, are splitting up, and it takes him a moment to realize she's serious. He feels himself groping for some fact, and she gives it to him. "Thirty-four years," she says, "they've been together. He's fifty-two and she's fifty-one." Wilson shakes his head as if to clear it. He feels something at the back of his throat, filling his chest. It's sorrow for her. He can feel his eyes prickling, and he blinks hard. He knows it's the drink, he knows it's nostalgia, some mutated self-pity, but still. She consoled him all those years ago, and now he leans in close, asks her how she's doing, and she gives a short laugh. She's been better. It's been bad. "I couldn't make sense of it for a long time. I wanted to punish them. I even threatened to stop them visiting their grandkids." She snaps a shot back and purses her lips. "I kept asking why, you know, why *bother*, and my mother got so angry. She's met someone else. She told me the way I looked at her it was as if her life was over, as if she couldn't change it." She pauses while the bartender fills their glasses. "And then I realized I was just angry at them. They're being so selfish. I kept thinking, what about me?"

"Well, what about you?" he says, and he takes her hand, and she lets him, but she says, "No. It's not like it was for you. You were a kid. I'm a grownup. I'm a mother, for crying out loud. It's not a tragedy. It's not the end of the world, really. How're you supposed to feel? I always thought you got through your teens and your parents were still together and you were safe somehow." She takes another shot and he matches her.

"Cheers," he says.

"Actually, you know how I feel?" she asks, her voice thick. "You really want to know?"

He tells her yes.

"I feel ridiculous." She is crying, and he puts his arm around her as she wipes the tears away and says again, "Ridiculous." She lays her head on his shoulder, and he worries for a moment that someone might catch them. But then he realizes there's no one left in his home town who knows him. No one except her. He smells her hair, and crazily, it's the same as sixteen years ago. He thinks of that time in bed. Touching her. It was the only time they were naked together. He remembers thinking how wonderful that was, to be naked with her, and how they had so much time, how they could wait for sex. He doesn't think either of them came that afternoon. They fell asleep, exhausted by desire, and woke in a panic to the sound of a door slamming downstairs. They dragged their clothes on like characters in a French farce, and he remembers almost laughing, not because it was funny but because he knew it would be, knew that they'd look back on it and it would be part of their history and they'd find it hysterical. *Do you remember when?* He was relieved that it was only her mother when they sauntered downstairs. He felt cocky, could hardly hide his grin, but she seemed preoccupied, too confused to notice. Mike had forgotten something at the store. If it had been him, Wilson thinks, he would have seen right through them.

Joyce excuses herself to go to the bathroom, and while she's away he thinks about reminding her of the story now, seeing if they can laugh about it, but he doesn't. He remembers something else. For two years afterward, until he lost his virginity

freshman year of college, he had thought of that moment, mas-
turbated to it, remained faithful to her.

When she comes back, she is weaving slightly.

"Boy," she says. "Get me out of here before someone sees me
like this."

In the car outside the bar, he kisses her. It makes her laugh,
and then she kisses him back. She tastes the same too, and the
memory is sharp. "Shall we drive somewhere?" she asks. Her
house is close — just a few blocks from her old home — but she
doesn't want to go back like this. Mike still lives at the old place
— she moved back, in fact, to be close to him — and he's sitting
for her. Wilson's a little unsteady himself, wants to park, and
without thinking about it does something they never did but he
always wished they had. He drives them to the outskirts of town,
to a small deserted lookout over Fresh Pond, the local lovers'
lane. The dark water is frozen. They recline the seats. There's
something about the childishness of it, the nostalgia of it, the
ridiculousness — he catches one of his belt loops on the hand
brake, she pushes the cigarette lighter in with her toe — that
makes it seem less serious, not like faithlessness, not like betrayal, not like sex, at least not until it's over and the car windows
are fogged and they pull their clothes on again. Or perhaps having started, neither of them has the heart to stop.

Afterward, they sit side by side, staring at the snow melting on
the windshield. Her hair clip rests on the dash where she must
have tossed it, the long curving teeth interlocked, like the fingers
of folded hands. He holds the steering wheel and tries not to
think. There is a hollow feeling in his stomach. He recognizes
this. It's a tendency he has to make a bad thing worse, to tip accident into tragedy, jump before the fall. Every so often a breeze

stirs the trees above them and a sudden shower of snow thumps hollowly onto the roof. Finally she says, "Well, that's one way to sober up." She needs to get back to her kids, and he starts the engine.

On the way, he says, "Unfinished business," and she says, "Yes," and what they both know is that it isn't unfinished anymore.

At her place she sits beside him for a few moments before going in. Wilson tells her he hopes it all works out. She nods. "The worst of it . . ." she says after a second. "The worst of it is that I always wondered about my parents. You know, when we were kids. I wondered about them, worried about them splitting up. They fought. A lot. When I was very young. Less when my sisters came along, but still sometimes with real hatred. It's one of the reasons I was drawn to you, I suppose. To see how bad it was. Only now," she says, "I wonder if they stayed together for us, my sisters and me. If we kept them together." She pulls her coat around her. "I guess it's not ridiculous I feel. It's guilty."

She looks across at him and he shakes his head.

"Parents," he says.

"And now I am one." She picks up her bag from between her feet, finds her keys. "If you don't want to turn into your parents, don't have kids, right?"

Cars shush past them on the pale street, snow piled on their roofs, six, eight, ten inches deep, like white luggage.

"Hey," he says quickly. "You know, I've always meant to ask." He actually blushes. "About us, what happened."

She plumps the bag on her lap, tells him she can hardly remember. "There was a fight. My mother and me. She thought you were dangerous, thought I'd get pregnant."

"What about your dad?"

"Stayed out of it, but then he always let her do the dirty work." She shrugs. "I told them I loved you"—and hearing her say it still gives him a strange thrill—"but even as I said it, I knew it wasn't true. In love with something, maybe. In love with love, but not each other."

Wilson lets it go. He isn't so sure, but he lets it go, and besides, they've had sex and it hasn't changed anything after all these years. He can still hear them when they lay together, him telling her he loved her, her telling him back. "We're so unoriginal," he'd said, and they had laughed.

She looks tired, exhausted.

"I've made things worse," he says, but she waves him off. "Just not better, huh?"

"You know," she says, looking at him sideways, "you don't have to compare everything. Your wife, me, our parents. Not everything's comparable."

"Right," he says.

"I'm happy," she says. "In my marriage. With my children. Really."

He's quiet.

"Children don't fuck up marriages," she says. "Grownups do. You didn't fuck up your parents' marriage. Just don't fuck up your own."

"That's a little ironic," he says.

"And you're a shit to say so."

"She's pregnant," he tells her back, and she stares at him for a long beat.

"Motherfucker," she whispers.

There's a moment of stillness—the engine ticks off slow seconds — and then they both burst out laughing, fall against each other, shaking.

"You've never done this before," she says when she catches her breath. "Have you?"

He wipes his eyes, shrugs.

"Well, take it from me, it's not the end of the world. Sex isn't the only thing holding you together. Some people fight more when they have kids. You know why? Because they can."

She leans over and kisses him chastely on the cheek. So that's it, Wilson thinks. It occurs to him that he has been looking for some kind of out, but now he knows he's going to have to carry this night, swollen as he feels with it, forever.

"Hey," she says suddenly, one foot already on the snowy sidewalk. "Could you do me a favor? Would you take Dad home? He usually walks, but you know, on a night like this . . . And I'm not really up for driving him myself."

"Okay. Sure," Wilson says. "If you think it's a good idea."

"Just don't tell him we fooled around."

"I wasn't planning on it. So long as he doesn't bring it up."

"That's settled, then." She opens her door fully, and a snowy gust sweeps into the car. "I won't invite you in. You'd just get cold, and a new face'll excite the kids if they're still up. Wait here and I'll send him out in a sec."

Wilson watches her go, but she doesn't turn back. He shivers in the lingering draft and then sniffs the air, rolls the windows down one by one, then up again. He sees Mike come out and flashes his headlights.

"Evening," the older man says, climbing in. His hair is fine and silvery blond, almost like a child's, and his heavy, lined face is raw from the cold or drink, Wilson can't tell which.

"How've you been keeping?"

"Can't complain," Mike says, buckling up. "Course, seeing you doesn't make me feel any younger."

"You're looking great," Wilson tells him.

"Yeah? Joyce said you'd turned out a charmer."

There's an awkward silence, and Wilson pulls away from the curb too quickly. He feels a momentary panic as the car fishtails in the fresh snow. Mike grasps his door handle and Wilson says, "Sorry." It reminds him of a statistical anomaly, and in his nervousness he starts on a story about how in some countries the accident rates increase after seatbelts are made compulsory. The theory being that people feel safer and therefore drive more recklessly. "No kidding?" Mike says. "There's even a proposal," Wilson tells him, wondering what his point is but pressing on, "a thought experiment really, suggesting that accident rates would drop if we sprayed the roads with ice and stuck sharp metal spikes to every steering column."

"How about that," Mike says, and then, politely, "This handles nice, though," as if the car were Wilson's and not a rental.

"Here we are already," Wilson says, cheerful with relief.

Mike thanks him for the ride. He releases his belt and it slithers over his shoulder. "I'll get the rest of your news from Joycey, I expect."

"It was good to see you again," Wilson says. "And Joyce," he adds after a moment, feeling like he's walking out onto the frozen Charles. But Mike doesn't bat an eyelid.

"You too. She says you've done well for yourself. A kiddie on the way too?"

"Yeah," Wilson says, and then, because something more seems expected, he surprises himself. "You know what worries me? It's crazy. I worry I'm going to treat her like a pet. Love her the way you love a dog or a cat or something."

Mike is looking down, tugging at his knuckles. "If only it were that easy," he says, with a slow grin. He puts a hand on Wilson's forearm and squeezes. "God bless."

Wilson waits until he sees him go inside, worried he'll slip in the snow, and then waits some more. He used to stand on this corner nights, he remembers, after he left them, before he walked back to his own home. He liked to watch the lights go on and off — the hall, the stairs, bathrooms, bedrooms. When he told Joyce once, she said it must look like the end of *The Waltons*. "Goodnight, Pa, goodnight, Ma, goodnight, John Boy." She thought it was funny, but it hurt him. He used to stand there and think about their future.

But now he knows with certainty that it was all already over when he heard that door slam, as they leapt up, struggled into their clothes, covered their nakedness, that it was already over when he thought they'd be laughing about it for years to come, that the door had been slammed too hard, that it wasn't someone coming home but someone in fury leaving. They'd been caught.

He thinks about Mike's face in the woods when he told him how he felt about his own parents' breakup. Mike married at seventeen, a father at eighteen. And it occurs to Wilson that if anyone kept Joyce's parents together, it was him.

He starts the car, begins to trace his way back through the white, familiar streets to his hotel. McGrath to Monsignor O'Brien Highway. But as he drives, another memory, something so oddly vivid he wonders if he dreamed it, comes back to him. Joyce was already asleep, but he had woken from a drowse, pulled the covers up and over his shoulder, and in doing so glanced at her body beneath them. It was a bright afternoon and the sunlight penetrated the comforter, so he could see her quite clearly. The sheets were rosy, a pastel shade he remembers distinctly because they were more girlish than she usually allowed herself to seem. He watched her for a moment in that warm, pink light, the soft folds surrounding her, watched her chest rising and falling with her breath, listened to her, fancying he could hear her heart — or was it his? — watched her curl into a loose ball, her knees tucked to her chest, her hands loosely cupped beneath her chin, and he was filled with a desire to protect her. And it was that desire, he thinks now, that filling, sweeping desire, that he first called love.

He finds himself driving faster, reckless in the snow, thinking about his wife and his about-to-be child. She'll be home soon, he calculates. It's almost late enough to call.

HOW TO BE AN EXPATRIATE

GO TO AMERICA. You love the books, the TV shows, the movies. Tell people you're tired of being a tourist and you want to live in a foreign country for a few months. You know, really live there. Tell your mother it's what you've always wanted. Remind your father how often he's said you should get out of England if you have the chance. Say it's only a master's degree. In American lit. One year.

Pack two suitcases and give away your guitar to a friend who plays it better than you anyway. Give away your TV and your tennis racket. Sit in the pub on your last night home and wish for any excuse — fire, flood, earthquake — not to go.

At Heathrow your father slips you five hundred dollars in cash that he's changed at the bank that morning. Then he warns you to look out for muggers. Give them the money, he says. Everyone has a gun over there. Your mother wants to make sure you've got your tickets and your passport. You say yes. She makes you show them to her. You are an only child, and sometimes you think your family takes this to mean you're only a child.

Tell your parents on the phone how much you like Boston. How friendly everyone is. The size of the portions in restaurants. Tell them you're happy, so they won't worry about you.

Hear the worry in your mother's voice. Marvel at how clear the line is. And how cheap international calls are from the U.S. Promise to call every week. Tell your father that you miss football. Tell him, "They call it soccer here." In the post the next week, receive a week's worth of cuttings from the sports pages of English newspapers. "What else do you miss?" your mother wants to know. Tell her you can't get English marmalade, but by the time some arrives in the post (which you now call the mail) you've found a little store in Faneuil Hall that stocks it. Don't tell her and continue to get a new jar of marmalade every month.

At night, lie awake listening to sirens — the distinctive American wail — and wonder if they're from the street or your neighbor's TV.

Walk the Freedom Trail. See the sites of historic importance. Realize you don't know any of the important history. Get bored and stop halfway. Go to Filene's Basement and the Bull and Finch Pub, the one *Cheers* is based on. The Bull and Finch doesn't look much like *Cheers* inside and doesn't feel like a real pub to you. You haven't been asked your age in a pub for years and you don't have a driving license and you don't feel safe carrying your passport everywhere. Have a Coke. Explain to your mother on the phone that they only use the outside of the pub on TV. Learn to call pubs bars. When you feel homesick, eat at McDonald's or Burger King or Kentucky Fried Chicken, just like at home. Think if anyone ever invents teleport booths, they should all be placed in fast-food joints around the globe to minimize the effects of immediate culture shock.

In the supermarket find jars of Coleman's mustard, Cross and Blackwell pickled onions, Lea and Perrin's Worcestershire sauce. Feel the tang of homesickness. Defend English food to your fellow students. Explain what Yorkshire pudding is. Complain that you can't get a decent curry in Boston.

Work out how much everything is in pounds. Phone calls are cheaper. Food is cheaper. Gas is cheaper than petrol.

At parties, people come up to you and ask you to say *weekend* or *schedule* or *Scottie Pippen*. Discover you can bring the house down by saying, "Whatchoo talking about, Willis?"

Drink a lot. American beer is weaker, and the bars stay open all night. Get a reputation as a drinker. Completely fail to explain to people why Budweiser was once fashionable in England. Smoke pot for the first time. Amaze your new friends with the fact that it's your first time. One of your fellow graduate students refuses to believe you. She lived in England for six months and she says she smoked pot. Be slightly annoyed that this person is telling you about your own country. Wonder how well you know your own country. She says words like *chemist* and *dustbin* and you share a taxi home with her. She is from New York, and you can hardly believe you're sleeping with a New Yorker. In bed you tell her you hear it's a wonderful town. "The Bronx is up," she observes, lifting the covers and sliding under them, "and the Battery down." Afterward, she lays her head on the pillow next to yours, whispers, "If you can make it there, you can make it anywhere."

"Do you have *Oprah*?" someone asks you, and you say, "Yes, we have *Oprah*. And *Cosby* and *L.A. Law* and *Baywatch*. And electricity and microwaves and indoor plumbing too. Just no guns and drugs." Get into stupid arguments. Insist that the movie *Glory* is a western, "maybe not geographically, but generically."

There is an election. You follow it with interest. It seems like a grand thing to be in another country during an election. When

Bill Clinton wins, you feel slightly superior to your friends in England, with John Major for prime minister. When they call or write and ask you how you like America, think of that map on election night. Say you like Boston fine but you don't know enough about the rest of America to judge: "It's like asking someone in London what they think of Vienna." Feel like an experienced traveler when you say this.

At Thanksgiving, call your parents and tell them, "It's Thanksgiving." Explain that it's just like Christmas, "except without presents or a tree." Spend the day with the family of the New Yorker. Her mother tells you she loves your accent. She knew a girl from England who was evacuated to the U.S. during the war. Maureen Johnson was her name. You nod, not that you know her, but as though you *might* know her. They ask you all about England, what you think of the Queen, Princess Di, Northern Ireland. Form some opinions. They tell you how much they admire Margaret Thatcher. You compliment the pumpkin pie. No, they don't have pumpkin pie in England. You tell your parents all this on the phone, and your mother says, "Americans are very hospitable, aren't they? I'm so glad they took you into their home." Feel suddenly like a refugee receiving charity.

You tell your parents that you're not coming home for Christmas. You want to experience an American Christmas. Break up with the New Yorker, just too late to buy a ticket home. On Christmas Day, spend forty bucks on the phone to your parents. Tell them how much you like America, so they won't worry. Listen to your father tell you how much your mother misses you. Listen to your mother tell you how much your father misses you. "All we want is for you to be happy," your mother says. Microwave the Christmas pudding they've sent you. Hope your father liked the Red Sox cap you sent him.

Discover that you're more popular with women than you ever thought. Ask them what they see in a bloke like you and make them laugh. You think they like your accent, these graduate students, and then you decide there's just a more mature approach to sex in the U.S. And then you realize it's because they're expecting you to leave the country in a few months. You're just a holiday romance. Sleep with them anyway.

Between girlfriends, when you are lonely, do a lot of academic work and in the spring get offered a Ph.D. place and a full ride. Fly home at the start of the summer to explain your decision to your parents. Bring live lobsters from Logan. Your mother says you look tired. Your father asks when you're going to get a job. "I thought you were only going for one year," he says. Take a deep breath. Tell them you don't want to fight. You're only home for a fortnight, shouldn't they make the most of it? In the silence afterward, listen to your lobsters scratching against their cardboard box.

In the days that follow, notice that instant coffee is undrinkable and that the service in Britain is terrible.

Back in the U.S., call and write to your parents, inviting them to visit. Tell them, "You don't have to wait for me to come there." Your mother says she'd like to, "but you know what your father's like." Call in the middle of the day with the news that you've had an article accepted for publication in a journal. "That's nice," she says, and tells you about her garden.

Go to an American football game. Tell your friends at the tailgate party how everyone in England admires American sports crowds because they're not hooligans. Your friends have brought something called a suitcase of beer, and you take turns smoking pot in the portable toilet. Get into the stadium and realize that you've never seen a crowd of drunker people in your life, but marvel at the absence of violence. Have this revelation: there's no crowd violence at American sports because there are only home fans. The country's just too big for fans to travel to away games. That's why so many sports are decided by series. Think, this is the kind of deep insight you came to the U.S. for.

Watch the Oscars live for the first time.

Manchester United, the soccer team you've supported since you were a kid, wins the Premiere League Championship for the first time in twenty-five years. You tell your American friends and they say, "Cool."

In the spring go to your first basketball game. In the summer go to your first baseball game. Nod your head knowledgeably about the Celtics and the Red Sox and the Patriots. Say, "So that's what a raincheck is." Learn to call them the Celts and the Sox and the Pats.

At the end of your second year, go home for Christmas. Sit in the departure lounge at Logan and feel oddly embarrassed for all the English people and then suddenly shy about your own accent. Sit in the pub at home and tell your friends about American girls, every British boy's fantasy. New York, California — these words in an English pub sound like sex. Let slip words like *fall* and *soccer* and have them make fun of you. Apparently you don't even sound like you anymore. Hear the way your tone goes up at the end of a sentence? Feel the anxiety of influence. Listen to them talk about bands and politicians and TV shows and sportsmen you've never heard of. When they say you look tired, say it's jet lag. Try to sound more English, and wonder if you're starting to talk like the Artful Dodger. Gor' blimey! Stone the crows! Lor' luv a duck!

Your best friend tells you you've changed. He tries to sound pleased, as if he told you so, but he looks at you as if it's a betrayal. Tell him, you should hope so. Tell him, didn't you go to the U.S. to change? Wasn't that the point? But later wish you'd asked him how you've changed. Wish you could be sure yourself.

In the pub on your last night home, call your friends "mates" and tell them, "Cheerio."

Meet a girl from California. Sleep with her and think, "She's from California." On your first date, she makes you wait in line for a table at a pizzeria in the North End. You'd never queue this long for fish and chips, but she says it's the best pizza in the world and you nod and listen to her tell you how the Mafia makes the North End safe by running off muggers and junkies. This makes about as much sense to you as queuing for pizza.

At the end of the summer, take her home to meet your parents. "Tell us about California," they say. They like her. She likes England. Wouldn't mind living there one day. This seems terribly attractive to you. Fall in love. Marry her. When your parents get off the plane to come to your wedding, they look smaller and older than you've ever seen them. They tell you your wife is lovely. They're really happy for you. They look scared in all the photographs.

Take your wedding album to the immigration interview. Tell the INS inspector how you met. Melt her heart. Get your green card and discover that it's pink. Your wife comes out of the interview looking a little pale. She says, how strange to think that her government could deny her something and she wouldn't have any rights. As if it weren't her own country. She is trembling slightly. Tell her everything's okay now. At the party to celebrate your new permanent-resident status, someone asks if you'll take citizenship. Say no. Say you can't imagine yourself swearing allegiance to any country. Tell your parents you're a legal alien. Never use the words *permanent resident* to them.

Lose track of how many months you've been in the U.S. Say eighteen months when it's been two years. Argue about it with your friends on the phone. Do well in your Ph.D. program. Have your parents tell you they're very proud. Explain your achievements to them carefully. Understand that to them, every success you have in your new country keeps you from going home. Have your professor write a glowing recommendation for a tenure-track position. Go out for jobs, even though you're still writing up and the chances are slim. Talk with your wife about moving back to Britain and getting a job. Remind her that she'd like to live there one day. What about her mother? she says.

Get a position in the U.S. In Wisconsin. Think about it for about two seconds. Accept it. Call your parents with the good news. "All we want is for you to be happy," your mother says. "I thought you were only going for one year," your father says. Call your best friend to give him the news. Have him tell you he's marrying his fiancée of two years, whom you realize you've never met.

Point out to your new academic colleagues wryly that *The Bridges of Madison County* was initially a flop in Britain, when it was published as *Love in Black and White*. But then, of course, it was reissued with a lot of hype and became a big hit. Wonder what your point is.

Realize one day that you haven't had any good marmalade in the mail for months.

Develop an interest in all things British. See every Anthony

Hopkins movie ever made. Reread Forster and Austen. Watch the Monty Python marathon. Quote from all these sources occasionally. Disagree with all the anglophile articles in *The New Yorker* but read them avidly. At Christmas your wife buys you a subscription to the foreign edition of a British newspaper. Your mother sends you a Manchester United shirt, which you put in your closet. Which you used to call a wardrobe. Write articles about Britain and the British. Say you had to leave to really understand your home.

Buy a car with a hood and a trunk rather than a bonnet and a boot. Say to your wife, "Do you call it a windshield or a windscreen?" Once when you've had a little too much to drink, swing onto the wrong side of the road. Your wife screams at you and you pull back. There's no real danger and you feel oddly elated.

Tell your wife you've noticed you're spelling words like *realize* with a *z*. Stare at her blankly when she says, "A zee? You mean a zed. A zee!" Ask her if she thinks you're losing your accent. Hear her say, "I don't *think* so."

When people ask you where you're from, start to say, "Originally?"

Be wary of other British people. Avoid them at parties. Feign surprise when your colleagues introduce you to their British graduate students. Say, "Oh, hello." They look pale and half starved. Notice how bad their teeth are.

Clinton's second election comes around and your wife goes to a rally. Remember how you used to be more political. How every little thing—roadworks, the homeless, Benny Hill—made you despair of Britain. Things like that in the U.S. are someone else's problem. Get a call from the Democrats. Can they count on your vote? Explain that you don't have a vote, that

you're not a citizen. Besides, you're not a democrat. You're a so-
cialist. It sounds so exotic. Forget to register for a postal vote in
the upcoming British general election.

The Patriots make the playoffs. Say, "That kid Bledsoe —
nothing but bullets." It makes people laugh at parties.

Your mother calls and tells you she's clearing out the attic. Do
you want to keep any of your old schoolbooks? Say no, you don't
think so. Not any? she says. Why not keep a couple? Say all
right. Your father comes on the other extension and tells you he's
sold your bicycle. You had been meaning to ship it over. Ask him
why. He says it was in the way, underfoot. "Clutter," he says. Ask
him what he got for it and get angry when he says, "Twenty
quid." It's only four years old and you paid over two hundred for
it. "I'm only kidding," he says quickly. "It's still here. But it's getting rusty. There's nothing I can do about that." Next time he
comes on the phone he pretends he's sold your books. Next time
he jokes about taking in a lodger in your old room. Next time he
says they're thinking of selling the house and buying something
smaller. Tell him, very funny. Tell him you're not laughing.
"Only teasing," he says.

When your mother calls, take the phone from your wife and
say, "How ya doing?" and feel like you've just slapped her in
the face. When your father calls, say, "What's up?" and groan
inwardly.

Lose track of how many years you've been in the U.S. Work it
out by administrations. Lose track of how many kids your best
friend has. Teach students Shakespeare. They look at you as
though you're an expert with your accent, although you know
their accents are closer to the Bard's. You call home every week
and write every couple of weeks. More often than any of your

old friends in England, you're sure. There isn't enough news for all these letters and phone calls. On the phone your mother tells you she and your father have fights about you. "He doesn't understand," she says. Tell her that you know what you're doing. That they shouldn't worry about you. Ask, is it because they miss you? Hear her say, "Oh, no." They're both busy and active, enjoying their retirement. She says it's not your fault. They'll have to get used to it. "I tell him, perhaps I should have had another child," she says. Neither of you speaks for a long moment. "I mean a *second* child," she says at last.

Cheat on your wife. She tells you one night you are losing your accent and it makes you feel like you're losing your hair. "Going, going, gone," she says. Cheat on her with a gifted student from your class. Cheat on her with less gifted students from your class. Talk to your oldest friend from England late at night on the phone. He's jealous of your affairs. "I could never do that," he says. You wonder if you could if you were there. "Have you been drinking?" he asks, and when you say "No!" he says, "Only it's six A.M. here."

A Starbucks opens around the corner from you, and you tell your wife, "Conformity. That's what I love about this country," and she calls you an asshole. Tell her you're an arsehole and watch her not laugh. Have a harassment suit filed against you by one of the students you didn't sleep with. Your wife wants a separation. She says, "Don't look so miserable. We've been together more than two years." She means that even if you divorce, you'll get to keep your pink green card.

"You've changed," she tells you, and you say, "I had to change to stay."

"You've changed," she says, and you ask, "How? Tell me how I used to be."

You've changed, and you wonder, too much or not enough?

Look at old photos. Reread letters. Wish you'd kept a diary. Think, you chose this. You're an expatriate, not an exile. It's what you always wanted.

At Christmas, after your wife leaves you, fly home for the first time in two years. You've spent winters in Boston when the Charles River froze solid and the snow was piled on street-corners into April, but you feel cold to your bones at Gatwick. Yes, you think, but it's a damp cold. The atrocious fucking coffee costs a fortune. Your parents have preserved your old room like a shrine for six years. They're delighted to have you home for Christmas. Your father slaps you on the back, and your mother's eyes fill with tears at the airport. "It's good to have you home," they say, although they insist they haven't missed you.

At night you lie awake in your old bed in your old room in your old home and you wonder how everything could have changed so much.

FROGMEN

MICHAEL AND JOHNNY
were playing deep-sea divers. They were on the embankment above the river with their cheeks blown out, making slow-motion swimming actions with their arms. Johnny was twelve and Michael was ten. They spoke in sign language and pointed down the bank whenever the masked head of one of the police divers emerged from the brown water.

Johnny stuck his thumb up and gestured that they should surface.

"Do you think they've found anything?" he said.

"No." Michael made treading-water movements. "Why aren't you sinking?"

"I'm hanging on to our boat," Johnny said.

"Well, move over. My arms are getting tired."

"Look," Johnny said, pointing behind his brother toward their house. A small pink figure was skipping across the field in a ballerina costume. "Susan," he said recognizing their six-year-old sister, but Michael had already taken a deep breath and puffed out his cheeks and sunk to his knees on the grass.

They tried to swim around Susan, but she just thought they were doing some kind of dance, and she stood on tiptoes and followed them around with her fingers laced over her head.

"What do you think of my new costume?" she said. "Isn't it

nice?" They kept swimming, but because they could only go in slow motion they couldn't get away from her, and she came twirling after them.

"Play with me," she called, but Johnny had his foot caught in a giant clam and was waving for help. Michael turned slowly to come to his aid, but Susan leaped in between them and gave a tug at Johnny's arm.

"Oh, what is it?" he said, sacrificing his last lungful of air.

"Dance with me," she said shyly.

"No way."

"You have to," she said. "I'm a ballerina. Mummy just bought me my costume."

"What for?" Michael asked.

"Will you dance with me if I tell you?"

"No."

"Will you?" she asked Johnny.

"Oh, all right."

"I just told her I was upset about Billy and so she bought it for me."

"You never did. You just told her that?"

"I did. She took me straight out to buy it. Just now."

Johnny looked at Michael.

"Are we going to dance now?"

"No. Get lost."

"But you promised."

"No, I never. Ask Michael. Did I say I promised?"

Michael shook his head.

"Did too," Susan said sulkily. She would have fought him then, but she didn't want to get her new costume dirty. "Well," she said with a huff, "you're just crap," and she scampered off toward the house.

Johnny waited until he saw their mother come out, then sat down in a heap.

"Look sad," he told Michael.

"Why won't you play with your sister, John?" his mother said angrily. He just looked up at her sorrowfully and pointed down the embankment. She looked and saw another masked head pop out of the water.

"Oh god," she said. "You poor babies," and she put her arms around both boys.

•

The Saturday after Billy Burns went missing, David's father took him to the toy department of Woolworth's and let him pick out two tennis rackets, one for himself and one for his best friend, Paul. When they got back, David raced over to Paul's house with the two rackets stretched out like wings, banking and making *ack-ack-ack* fighter-plane noises. Paul's mother had bought him boxing gloves that same morning, but only one pair. The boys took one each, and using the tennis rackets as swords, they dueled and punched their way up and down the garden until David's mother called him in for dinner.

Martin got a kite in the shape of Batman, but he couldn't get it off the ground and his father had to come out and fly it for him. Every time Martin took the string, the kite plunged to earth, so in the end his father made him run into the house for some paper. "We'll send a message to Batman," he said, tearing a hole in one of the sheets of paper. He threaded it onto the string, flicked it once, and the wind caught it and carried it up to the kite. After that, he had Martin sit at his feet and write messages to the kite. "Where's Robin?" Martin wrote. "Why do you wear your underpants over your tights?" he wrote. "Can you see

Billy Burns?" Each message made the kite heavier, and gradually Batman sank to the ground. Cathy, from down the street, brought it back to them on her new roller skates.

Johnny and Michael got new Action Man dolls. Their mother asked them if they were sure that's what they wanted — in her day, dolls were for girls — but they said yes, it was what they'd always wanted. Didn't they both have Action Men? she asked, but they very patiently explained that they had old Action Men with plastic hands.

"New Action Men have gripping hands," Johnny said.

"They're made of rubber," Michael added. "So they can hold guns and things better."

"I never knew it was so complicated," their mother said.

Really old Action Men had plastic hair, they told her, before they had bristles.

"It's like Action Man's been growing up, then?" Their mother laughed.

Well, no, they said. They thought he'd always been about the same age.

"And when did Action Man get his scar?" she wanted to know.

"Mother," said Johnny, "Action Man has always had a scar."

"John," his mother mimicked, "aren't you getting a little old for this?"

•

Billy Burns, as Johnny and Michael both knew, had had a new Action Man with gripping hands. He'd got it for his twelfth birthday. Billy had always had the best toys. He had tried to swap his old Action Man with Johnny for a magnet, but Billy's mother had made them swap back, even though they'd shaken on it. "It wasn't a fair swap," she'd said, but Johnny didn't see how that mattered if Billy had agreed to it. It never occurred to him that he might have bullied Billy into it. You couldn't bully someone older than you.

Just wait till I show her I've got my own now, Johnny thought.

At the time Billy had said he was sorry and he really preferred the magnet, but the Action Man was a present from his father and his mother said he had to keep it. Billy's father had "vanished" the year before. "No one knows where he is," Billy had told them. "He's a spy or something." Johnny didn't believe that, but he didn't ask anymore about Billy's father, because his parents had told them he shouldn't. Only after Billy disappeared, he wondered if this was something you inherited, and he asked his mother if Billy had vanished like his father.

"No," his mother said. "Billy's father hasn't vanished. He just decided to go away. Billy didn't want to go anywhere. He's lost."

"Maybe he ran away," Johnny said. "Maybe he didn't like it at home and he just ran away."

"Don't say that," his mother said, and he thought she was angry until she pulled him tight against her.

Once, Johnny remembered Billy coming to the door and saying, "Do you notice anything different about me?" and Johnny had wondered if he should say, "Yes. You don't have a dad," but he didn't. "No," he said, and then Billy smiled and unzipped his coat and showed him where he had strapped his cowboy holster under his shoulder. "See," he said. "Now we can play detectives."

•

The police were gone from the river when Johnny and Michael got back to the embankment with their toys. They played commandos for a while. They imagined Action Man swimming into the German harbor past all the mines and nets and blowing up the ships. They imagined Billy doing that, with a knife in his teeth, swimming past all the policemen to the sea. They were interrupted by Susan again. She came running out with a strange dog leaping and barking around her heels.

"Where'd you find him?" Johnny said, jumping up.

"Do you like him?"

"Yeah," they chorused.

"Well, he's mine," she said. "Daddy bought him for me."

"What?"

"I told him I was upset about Billy and that Mummy bought me an outfit and that she was taking you to town to buy whatever you wanted. But no one ever said I could have *whatever* I wanted. Mummy just said she'd get me the costume, so it wasn't really fair. So Daddy asked me what I most wanted."

"A dog," Johnny said, in awe. "How did you think of a dog?"

"Well, I asked for a pony first," Susan said.

"What's he called?" Michael wanted to know.

"Billy, of course."

And they chased him off down the field behind the houses, shouting, "Billy! Here, Billy — here, boy." That brought out all the parents down the street, theirs and David's and Paul's and Martin's and Cathy's. Only Mrs. Burns stayed indoors. Their father grabbed Johnny and Michael by the shoulders and shook them hard. Their mother caught Susan by the arm and smacked her bare legs until she cried.

•

Susan told. She said it had all been Johnny's idea to get the presents. She showed her brothers her legs, still red from smacking, and said she had to. But she got to keep Rover, as he was now to be called, while Johnny and Michael had to go and apologize to Mrs. Burns and take their toys and say they were presents for Billy when he got home. "He already has one," Johnny hissed at his father, but it was no good. Mrs. Burns took their offerings without a word, but Johnny's father must have seen something in her face, some gleam of hope. By the end of the week every family in the close had sent her a present for Billy. The local paper picked the story up, and before long presents were arriving from all over town. A local bicycle shop even donated two bikes of different sizes so that Billy would never outgrow them.

Johnny sat with Michael and Susan and David and Paul and Martin and Cathy on the wall opposite the Burnses'. For days they watched strange cars pull up and prim children in shirts and ties or party dresses whom they'd never seen before go up to the door with armfuls of gaily wrapped presents. None of them said a word. They were all lost in their thoughts, dreaming of the piles of toys behind the door.

"We'll never see them again," Johnny said to himself.

•

The best toy Billy Burns ever had, in Johnny's opinion, was his camera. It wasn't a "proper camera," as Billy was the first to admit—it didn't take normal film, just single plates—but it came with all the chemicals to develop pictures. "Like a cross between a camera and a chemistry set," Billy had said when he got it the Christmas before. No one was really very interested until Michael found the dirty magazine. It had been floating in the river and got stuck on the bank. "Hey," he'd shouted, and Johnny and Billy had jumped on him and twisted his arm behind his back. They'd been playing detectives and Michael had been the murderer, but when he'd found the magazine he'd forgotten he was supposed to be hiding.

"No," he said as they marched him up the bank. "I'm not playing anymore. There's something back there you should have a look at."

"You don't really expect us to fall for that old one, do you, chump?" Johnny said, poking him in the ribs with his six-shooter, but when they finally got him back to the base and tied him up, they listened to him.

"It could be evidence," Billy decided.

"We shouldn't touch it," Johnny said, thinking of germs and fingerprints, and that's when he told Billy to fetch his camera. Leaving Michael tied up — he said he'd tell on them, but they ignored him because he was younger than them and their prisoner — the two older boys went down to the water's edge. The girlie magazine was half hidden in a tangle of nettles. Johnny turned the pages with a stick and Billy took photographs of all the bodies stretched out across them. Back in Billy's bathroom, they watched him tipping the tray of chemicals back and forth, making waves across the plates. Johnny wanted a go, but then the pictures began to develop and he forgot to ask. The dark patches of hair surfaced first, and then the eyes, and then the rest of the body. It was like watching someone in the bath, Johnny thought, when the plug was pulled out. None of them said anything. Not even Michael, with his hands still tied behind him. They watched Billy develop picture after picture.

They'd had to hide them quick when they heard Billy's mother come in, and afterward, when Johnny asked him what he'd done with the photos, Billy told him he'd burned them.

"Why?" Johnny had demanded, suddenly furious.

"I was bored," Billy said.

"I don't believe you."

"Don't then. They burned great."

Johnny didn't know what to say to that. He'd always thought of himself as the leader, even though Billy was nine months older. It made him feel strange to think of Billy burning the pictures alone, without telling anyone.

When Billy went missing, a policewoman asked all the children if they could think of anything that might help find him. "Did anyone ever see Billy playing by the water?" she asked, crouching down to look in their eyes. All Johnny could think of was the magazine and the pictures. He thought if he opened his mouth he'd blurt it out, so he kept his lips pressed together and shook his head when it was his turn to answer. "Nothing at all?" the policewoman asked him, and he shook his head again. He gave Michael a look across the room, and when it was his turn he did the same.

•

Days went by and there was still no sign of Billy. Johnny's parents forbid him and Michael to play near the water, but the police divers had moved downstream by now, following the river to the coast, so the boys didn't mind. People began to whisper that Billy wasn't coming back. Johnny thought of the toys and said to himself, *What a waste.*

Billy's father did reappear briefly in the second week. The children watching from the wall wondered if he was also going to be hidden away in the house as an incentive for Billy to come home, but he came out within an hour and got back in his car and drove off. The local paper said he was staying in a nearby hotel, waiting for word.

Johnny remembered the week that Billy's father had "vanished." It had been his and Billy's first week at school in long trousers. He remembered his mother telling him what had happened and waiting for Billy in the playground one morning, meaning to say something. Their friends David and Paul asked him what they should do and Johnny said, "We should say how sorry we are, that's all," but when they thought of saying it, and of the serious grown-up faces they would have to pull, they just looked at each other and fell about laughing.

That was also the first week they had a proper games class at school. Before, they had just taken their sweaters off and put on trainers and gone out on the field. Now they had to go to the changing rooms and put on their nylon running shorts and their new white T-shirts. On their first day their teacher, old Mr. Robinson, told them to change while he set out equipment in the gym. But when he came back they still weren't ready. "Get a move on, you lot," he said. "You'll waste half the period at this rate." They all went so slowly because they were shy. A wave of nervous laughter passed from one cubicle to the next as they looked at one another's pale hairless bodies. Johnny turned sideways while he undressed, but Billy just laughed. "I can see you," he said. Johnny didn't say anything, but he couldn't help noticing the thin dark hairs curling around Billy's privates.

•

Finally, one evening at the end of the second week, Mrs. Burns came to her door. The children playing in the street stopped what they were doing to watch her. She beckoned them. No one moved. She pointed at each of them in turn and crooked her finger, but no one went to her. Then she looked at Johnny and he heard someone call out, "He's the oldest." He didn't want to, but he took a step forward in case anyone should think he was scared. He went right up to the door, ready to turn on his heels in a second, and stood there. Mrs. Burns looked him up and down, reached behind her, and put a parcel in his hands. When he turned round, the others were beginning to form a line.

She gave out toys to all of them. They could take as many parcels as they wanted, but of course no one knew what was in them, and no one would open the boxes in front of Mrs. Burns. Girls and boys spent the whole night swapping back and forth. Johnny got a book that he already had and Michael got a cowboy hat too small for him. They kicked through the piles of wrapping paper as if they were leaves, looking for their Action Men. In the end they found three and not two.

"One must be Billy's," Michael whispered. "I can't tell which." They looked around at all the children running up and down the street brandishing new toys and wondered how many other of Billy's things were mixed in with the new presents. "Don't touch anything," Johnny told his brother, and they slowly backed out of the wrapping paper.

•

Johnny was at school when the police made the official announcement. A special assembly was called, and all the pupils lined up in their forms. Johnny could see Michael two ranks in front of him, and the other children, David and Paul and Martin, around him. On the far side of the hall would be Cathy, and right at the front his sister, Susan.

Mr. Johnson, the headmaster, had put on the black gown he

normally wore only for prize-givings. "Batman," Johnny muttered under his breath, and then, "Pass it on," but no one did. Mr. Johnson told them that William Burns's body had been found washed out to sea. Billy had drowned.

That evening there was a big picture of Mrs. Burns on the front page of the newspaper, with a smaller one of Billy beside it. Johnny thought she looked old, and he was glad she wasn't his mother. Johnny's father read from the newspaper that she was going back to Scotland, where she had family, and that the funeral would be in Glasgow.

"Will they bury him or cremate him?" Johnny asked.

"It doesn't say."

"I think I'd prefer to be cremated," Johnny said, and his mother said, "John!"

There had been a reporter outside the gates at the end of school, and there were quotes in the paper from some of the children in Johnny's class.

"Didn't they ask you?" his father said, and Johnny lied and said, "No."

The reporter had pushed his tape recorder toward Johnny and asked him what Billy was like, but the man couldn't hear him over the other kids, thrusting up their hands and calling, "Me! Ask me!"

"What was that, son?"

"He was all right," Johnny repeated. "I said he was all right." But the reporter was already turning away.

•

The school organized a memorial service at the local church for the children and their parents, and that was where Mr. Johnson announced that there would be extra swimming lessons on Saturdays. Mr. Robinson and all the other teachers who could swim had agreed to come in and work for nothing to teach everyone how. The boys in Johnny's year were scheduled to start their class that Saturday at 9 A.M. They would be first.

On Friday night, Johnny lay in the bath. He studied himself for a moment, then leaned back and slid down until the warm water lapped under his chin. He closed his eyes, but only for a second, to see what it was like. The water was hot, and he felt the sweat beading on his forehead. It was odd, he thought, that you could sweat in the bath. He closed his eyes again and sank down until the water almost touched his lips. He felt a wave run over his stomach and stir the hair that lapped around his privates.

Downstairs he heard Michael complaining loudly that he would miss Saturday morning cartoons "because of stupid swimming." Someone tried to open the door, and his father said, "John? Why have you locked this door?"

"I'm fine," he said, sitting up so fast the tub squeaked. "Just a second."

When his mother came up to kiss him goodnight, Johnny told her, "I always wanted to learn, really," and she said, "Good. There's a big boy."

•

Johnny's class went into the changing rooms at 8:55, undressed, and put on their trunks. Johnny placed his by his feet so that when he pushed his trousers down, he needn't look around for them.

"Don't worry, lads," Mr. Robinson said. "It's the easiest thing in the world." At nine o'clock sharp, he led them out and lined them up along the edge of the shallow end, where the water was only four feet deep.

"When I blow the whistle," he said gently, "I want you all to hop in smartish."

They stood there and shivered while their parents and the next class sat and watched from the benches on one side. People's voices sounded funny in the pool, echoey, so they talked very quietly. Johnny curled his toes over the edge of the tiles. He looked to one side and saw his parents, with Susan on his mother's lap and Michael standing between his father's legs. He looked down the row of boys and saw David and Paul and Martin all looking ahead.

Then the whistle blew and he began to cry.

EQUAL LOVE

DIXON WAS MAKING COF-
FEE, listening to the spit and splutter of the percolator, waiting
for his best friend's wife to come downstairs. That sounded bad,
he thought, but he tried to remind himself that nothing bad,
nothing terrible, nothing *irretrievable* had happened yet. He
looked out the kitchen window, down the long garden into the
trees beyond. It was March, spring break, and his best friend and
his best friend's wife had come to visit for the first time in almost
two years. They'd come east for a cultural anthropology conference in the city — a series of mediocre panels on rites of passage,
according to the best friend — then driven up to Dixon's place in
rural Maine for a couple of days.

Dixon had cotton mouth. They'd drunk two bottles of wine
the night before, mostly him and his best friend's wife. Dixon's
own wife had a class this morning — they both taught at the
local state college, she English, he psychology — so she'd turned
in early, and his best friend never drank much. His wife —
the best friend's — liked to tell a story of him throwing up on
their first date, explaining how he lacked the enzymes to break
down alcohol. "She makes me sound dickless," the best friend
complained mildly. "Someone has to drive," he added — an old
line — although no one had had to drive last night. It slightly

annoyed Dixon, his. friend's reticence with drink, the way he would sip at a glass of red for hours, finally get bored, and dump it into his wife's glass. The driving thing was a joke, but not just a joke. The best friend gave off this aura of readiness, as if he were raring to take someone to the hospital, the all-night pharmacy, the airport. As if he and not they were ready for disaster, the designated cool head. "Driving, remember?" the best friend said with a smile when Dixon offered him another, and the best friend's wife pretended she held an imaginary steering wheel in her hands. "Driving," she mimicked, crossing her hands, making the sound of screeching tires. "Driving where?" And the best friend said dramatically, "Who knows?" as if nothing could surprise him, nothing could catch him off guard. And in fact many years before, the best friend had been the only one sober enough to take Dixon's daughter to the emergency room when she woke up late one night with an acute ear infection.

Dixon poured wine for himself and an almost brimful glass for his best friend's wife to kill the bottle. Dixon had known his best friend since college, but they'd barely been acquaintances then. It was only when they'd met again in graduate school, each part of an established couple, that they'd become close, become each other's first adult friends (so they'd congratulated themselves), learned to measure their relationships and then their marriages against each other's. Dixon wondered how long his best friend had irritated him, and if he'd be his best friend if, in fact, Dixon had any other friends at all.

Dixon sometimes wondered about his friend, wondered who had done better. Perhaps it evened out, he thought. His own wife was quite successful, after all, and he felt a flush of slightly drunken pride in her. The best friend's wife had never finished her Ph.D., never worked since their baby was born except occasionally as an adjunct teacher. But then it occurred to him that perhaps his friend had done better *because* of his wife's situation. He'd been able to move on, take jobs at better universities, while Dixon and his wife had stayed put, found it too hard to move when they would both need new jobs. Now that Dixon thought about it, his best friend's wife hadn't finished her Ph.D. precisely *because* they'd moved for the best friend to take his first job. Come to think of it, Dixon realized, that was when they had married, the best friend and his wife. "I couldn't very well ask her to give all that up and move halfway across the country with me unless I married her," he recalled his best friend saying.

Dixon and his own wife had stayed on until they both finished grad school. They'd had a couple of bad years right after they married when there'd been no money. Maybe *they'd* married as an insurance against those tough years. He recalled a pair of baggy mauve sweatpants his wife had owned. He used to make fun of her in them, call them her pink pants and her the Pink Pantster, sing the song from the cartoon: "Well, here she is, the Pink Pantster, the rinky-dink Pantster. Was there ever a Pantster so pink?" He thought he was being hilarious, and then one day she burst into tears and told him it was hateful, and he had found himself frozen halfway toward a gesture of comfort by the thought that he did hate those pants, hated that his wife had to wear ugly old pants and couldn't afford to throw them out.

After the wine, after his own wife had gone up and the kids, Dixon's boy and his best friend's daughter, had finished watching TV and said goodnight, Dixon brought out the Scotch—an inch of Oban and a new bottle of Longmorn the best friend had bought him. Dixon's daughter came home around eleven after a

movie, rolled her eyes at the empty bottles. Dixon had to resist
the urge to cup his shot glass, hiding it in his big hands. "Kids
today," she said, and the best friend, her favorite, called out,
"Mom!"

Finally, around one, Dixon sneaked into the downstairs bathroom and found his last few desiccated buds of pot in an old film
canister. He shook it beside his ear and then set it, with a grin at
the other two, on the table between them. It had been so long —
years — he didn't even have rolling papers, but the wife — the
remaining wife, his best friend's wife, not his own — was into
it. She disappeared upstairs to the guest room and came back,
smug, with a tampon wrapper. It lay on the table, curling slightly
until Dixon thought *What the fuck* and began to roll a joint. He
paused for a second when he'd rolled it, gathered his spit, ran
his tongue along the flap, and pasted the thing together, and
really — "No, *really*," he said — it didn't look so bad. "Wish me
luck," he told them, surprised to find himself whispering. He
went back into the downstairs bathroom to light up. It was too
bright in there — in the mirror his eyes looked hooded and his
face puffy; he had a zit on his temple — and too noisy with the
din of the fan, but it was where he allowed himself to smoke. At
forty-five, he was long past the irony of having once hidden his
smoking from his parents and now hiding it from his children.
I laugh at irony, he told his image in the mirror, narrowing
his eyes, not at *the* irony but at the emptiness of irony, at the
very irony of irony. And yet he knew too he was afraid of being caught by his kids, hadn't done this in so long because of
them, only felt safe now with his friends here. Behind the fan,
he thought he heard voices, faint, indistinct, unintelligible —
speaking to him or overheard, he couldn't tell.

The tampon wrapper worked surprisingly well, and he had taken a couple of long tokes when there was a knock at the door. It was his best friend and his best friend's wife. "How is it?" they asked, and he grinned hugely, held it out. The best friend shook his head. "I'm beat. I'll see you in the morning. Play nice." He kissed his wife, and when they parted Dixon found that he was staring. The best friend gave him a look and lunged forward, planted a smacker on his forehead. "Je-sus!" Dixon cried and then, immediately, "Shh!" And when he realized he was the one making the noise, complained, "You're letting the smoke out."

"Two words," the best friend said, holding up a finger, putting it to his lips. "Toxic shock."

His wife plucked the joint from Dixon's grasp, waved her husband away. "Drive safe," she whispered.

When his friend was gone, Dixon lay back against the wall to give her space to slip in and pull the door shut. "Shit," she said, squinting in the glare from the smooth white walls. "I'd get these stuccoed if you're planning on spending a whole lot of time in here." They stood together, passing the joint back and forth. It was hard to talk over the white noise of the fan, so they stared at each other — a blinking contest — until he looked away and met her eyes in the bright, shiny mirror. She toyed with the little bowl of potpourri his wife had set on the counter. She sniffed her fingers, held them out to him. "Nothing," he mouthed, shaking his head.

She pinched the stub of the joint, took a long toke. "Whoo!" she gasped, passing it back to him. She sat down on the toilet lid, thought better of it after a moment, and stood again, smoothing her skirt.

"It is a little sordid, don't you think?" she asked him.

He sucked at the end of the joint, offered her the last of it, but she shook her head. "Reminds me of masturbation," he said, tossing the spent roach into the bowl and flushing. He regretted saying it immediately, but she laughed throatily. "Yike," he whispered, shaking his head. He had a fleeting image of his son, the boy's look of fear when Dixon had tried to talk to him about sex, a look he suddenly recognized as contempt. He opened the door to let her out, pulled it closed behind him with the fan still beating.

Afterward Dixon and his best friend's wife sat up on the couch watching TV and finishing their Scotch. She tipped her glass back until the ice clacked and slid against her nose. Dixon flipped channels until he came to a soft-porn show on cable — fetishists on all fours wearing leather bridles, g-strings with horse tails, straddled by riders with crops. They laughed at it together, the comedy of sex, the light, weird entertainment of it, bumping shoulders, leaning against each other, and finally, in the course of things, kissing.

●

Dixon heard footsteps above, over the sound of the coffee, and knew that his best friend's wife was up. His own wife had climbed out of bed two hours earlier — she'd left the clock radio playing NPR — and he'd heard his best friend offer to drive her to work and then take Dixon's daughter to the mall. Dixon's wife didn't like to drive, and his daughter doted on the best friend, had been flirting with him ever since she was a toddler. They'd had a game back then, the tiny girl running, tottering with excitement, through the friend's spread legs, shrieking with pleasure. Dixon kept calling it the Tunnel of Love until his friend quit it. He still felt the need to tease his daughter about her crush, but the result was that she found ways of spending time with his best friend without him. He'd stumbled downstairs with a bad case of bed-head, which his daughter had mocked and his wife had failed to smooth down, in time to watch them, blearily, walk down the path to the car. It had struck him how much his daughter, taking his friend's hand, resembled his wife—the set of her shoulders and neck, her thin, springy legs. "You're so lucky," his friend had told him when she'd been born, the first child to any of them, and Dixon had been moved by his envy.

He wondered for a second about his own wife, her fidelity. Would she ever? Might she be tempted? But he was confident of her love. He recalled a moment years ago when he'd been in a car with his wife and his best friend's wife—though neither of them were wives then. Perhaps they'd dropped his friend off. Perhaps they were going to pick him up. But no, it felt late, in his memory, as if they'd left him. They'd been drinking already too, because the girls, the not-yet-wives, were talking about boys, and his girl, his soon-to-be wife, said, "I love the way he smells," and Dixon, who'd been watching the road carefully because he'd had a little too much to drink, realized slowly that she meant him. He teased her for years about it. But when he thought about it now, what was special was the way she told it to the other, the other proto-wife. She had said it to him before, when they were alone, but said to someone else it had a different, thrilling force. He knew she loved him, because she said it like that, because she couldn't stop herself, because it was too big for just the two of them to know.

He was staring at the empty bottles from the night before, rinsed and upended to dry in the rack, when his son and his best friend's daughter came clumping through the kitchen, the boy in a fatigue jacket, the girl in a yellow slicker, on their way to the rink across the park. He told them to have breakfast, but they were in a hurry, and he contented himself with reminding them to be back in time for lunch. The girl called him Uncle, and his son laughed at her. He watched them cross the back yard and head off through the woods, and then he watched the trees.

Nothing had happened beyond the kissing the night before, beyond their both knowing they'd like sex and agonizing about how terrible it would be. But they'd done the right thing. Dixon was glad of it, and when his best friend's wife appeared he saw from her face that she knew it was for the best too. It was an awkward moment. He wasn't sure if they would ever refer to it, and he thought he'd let her decide. She was in a jade-green bathrobe of his wife's, with her hair up in a towel, and she looked tired.

"Coffee," she croaked, like a man in a desert, and he poured and sat with her at the breakfast table. She licked her lips and he smiled.

"Me too."

Outside they heard the percussive *bap* of a basketball on the sidewalk approach and recede.

"Tell me you hear that too," he said. "It's not just in my head."

She smiled, and it made her look haggard, though whether from fatigue or anxiety he couldn't tell.

"Getting old," she said, as if reading his mind, a litany between the four of them for years, a sour punch line to so many of their discussions about the children, their students. But this morning in the buttery sunlight cutting through the kitchen blinds, he saw it was true. Her pale skin was wrinkled and bruised-looking beneath the eyes, and her always slightly mannish features looked heavy. He recalled a moment, a phrase of his best friend's, tried to place it—back in grad school, in a bar when the best friend still drank, or tried to, just the two of them certainly, but maybe later, after the children: *"She puts the dog into dogged."* He hadn't thought of it in years, and it made him feel suddenly awful to know it, to hear again the old and probably long-forgotten bitterness of it, but mostly to have carried it as a secret for so long, a secret for his best friend, from his friend's wife. To carry the simple power to hurt. He sat quietly, trying to quell the terrible, choking feeling that he might just blurt it out.

He found himself staring at her bare calf where it swung beside the table, delicately veined, the skin shiny, the flesh soft but a little loose. He wanted to reach out and grip it tightly. He remembered her lips—full and smooth but with that slight waxiness before chapping—and he was filled with an overwhelming sense of pity. Not that she wasn't still good-looking, he thought, out of a kind of fierce loyalty, but it made him feel foolish, more foolish for last night, more foolish than on the nights he sat up alone, awake, thinking of his most attractive students—their casual, studied appeal. It seemed dumber to risk everything for this, less real somehow, less serious.

"Sleep okay?" he asked her, and she nodded.

"Just not enough. You?"

"Yeah."

"No regrets?"

"No," he said carefully. "You?"

"Rien." Her tongue fluttered against the roof of her mouth, rolling the *r*.

"The sleep of the just," he said, but she seemed distracted, listening to the grind and slap of a skateboard pass in the street.

"I hope you know," she said at length, "it wasn't anything to do with you. If things were different . . . Well. I'd be lying if I said it hadn't crossed my mind."

He smiled, not sure whether to be hurt, not sure whether he'd rejected her or she him. But after all, he thought, wasn't this inevitable for every friendship between two couples: that a partner in one would speculate about a partner in the other?

"More than once," she said. "Over the years."

"*Moi aussi.*" He was trying to be flippant, but his accent, he realized, was atrocious. He felt like a boy whose voice had just broken. Something was happening, he thought, and perhaps because he had thought the danger was past, perhaps out of relief, perhaps because he felt he'd done what could be humanly expected, because they'd already *done* the right thing, he said, "They're all out," and she said, "Yes. Yes, they are."

They kissed then for several minutes in the kitchen, in full view of the windows, until the fear of being seen lent him urgency and he pulled her away. He led her up the stairs, putting his hands under her robe, shocked at her warmth. Her skin was still damp and slightly tacky from her shower, and his hands wouldn't slide over her. There was a moment of indecision at the top of the stairs, his — *their* — room, the faint strains of public radio still drifting from it, or the guest room? But she seemed to sense it, pressed herself against him. And it occurred to him to take her here on the landing, between all the rooms of the house, all the doors, and he told her to wait and ran into his bedroom and found a blanket. The radio was playing jazz and he rolled the volume up. He was coming back to her, aware that any second's pause might end this, but at the last minute he thought of a pillow for her. It was a kind thought, loving, domestic, the type of thought that made him think he was still a good person, and for a second he was absurdly comforted by it. Back in the room, bending over the bed, taking his pillow, he paused, stooped, his erection pressing against his pants, and looked out the window to the trees, saw a movement, a flash of something yellow. At first he thought it might just be a trick, the constant swaying of the blinds in the rising heat from the baseboards. But there it was again. His best friend's daughter, her slicker open, flapping, and his son. And he felt a flutter of something in his chest, felt a dizziness, put out a hand to steady himself.

When he was calm he called her to him, and she slipped gingerly into the bedroom and crouched with him, one hand on his back as they watched the children: the boy, twelve, the girl — what? Dixon couldn't quite recall; twelve or thirteen, though. He remembered his best friend and his wife doting on Dixon's baby daughter. "You've inspired us," his best friend had said. Their daughter had been born two years later, Dixon's son six months after that. Now the children walked arm in arm, staggering a little against each other, swinging their skate bags in their free hands, and just before the treeline they stopped and the girl leaned up against a birch and the boy pressed against her — for a paralyzed second Dixon wondered what he was doing — and kissed her, a long kiss, so long Dixon felt himself redden, conscious of the indecency of watching but unable to turn away, a kiss not even interrupted when the boy shifted to press his hand against the girl's small chest. And when it was over, finally, Dixon felt young — or at least, as he would think of it later, newly, freshly, *vibrantly* old — and the woman beside him, his best friend's wife, patted his back and said, "Oh!" and then, "Well," and then finally, "Oh, well," and they straightened, shakily, guiltily, blushing, and went down to greet their glowing, lying children.

SALES

MY EARLY RETIREMENT came about after one of my customers wanted to cancel her order. Mrs. Kidner, her name was. Got on very well, we did, too. She looked about my age—going a little gray—but she must have been younger, because she was raising a little girl. On her own and all. I remember thinking she'd have dyed that hair if she'd still been married.

Anyhow, she talked and talked about this girl. My darling this and my darling that it was, and there were pictures of her all over the house, even one of those pretend oil paintings they make from a photo in a big gilt frame. "I wish you could meet her," Mrs. Kidner went. "She'll be so sorry to have missed you."

"I feel like I know her already," I said.

She made me tea and sandwiches and she even took me upstairs and showed me the little girl's room. She opened the cupboard doors and the chest of drawers and showed me all her clothes folded away. It seemed a bit funny, but I had to admit she kept a very neat room. "Not like my lad's," I said.

I told her I could come back another day if she'd like me to talk about the encyclopedia with her girl, but she said, "Oh no, Mr. Robson." I liked that. "Oh no, *Mr.* Robson. That won't be necessary. I couldn't bring you all the way out here again. Besides, I've already made up my mind." She signed an order for the most expensive leather-cased set with a commemorative page bound in the front of the first volume: "To my daughter, Mary, on her twelfth birthday, from her loving mother."

When I went into the office the next week, there'd been a call from Mrs. Kidner's son. Her grown-up son, that is. It seems she isn't all there. Bit gaga, you might as well say. Turns out her daughter was knocked down and killed nine years ago.

•

I used to be famous around the office as the only salesman who actually read the encyclopedia. The other lads took the Mick something rotten. "What page are you up to now, Robbo, you sad bastard?" "Four hundred and sixty," I'd say, or "Seven hundred and eighty-eight," or "A thousand and forty-frigging-five." And when they started throwing paper, I'd stand up and put my hand on my heart and say, "Know your product, boys. Know your product."

I started reading it for my lad, Kevin. He was just a nipper then, asking me all these awkward questions. "Why is the sky blue? What makes the sun shine?" My wife, Beth, just stood there laughing. "Go on then, Tom. Tell him. You spend every waking hour with those books of yours. Can't you answer a simple question for your son?" And you know, I really wanted to have all the answers. For him, like. More than anything I'd ever wanted. So I started reading up on things, and that's how I found that it helped with my selling if I was able to tell people that my boy and I used the encyclopedia ourselves.

People look at you like you're a magician if you tell them you're a salesman. They think you're going to sell them something if they're not careful, like pulling a coin out of their ear. You can tell them water's wet, in that mood, and they won't believe you. It's the most awful thing about the job when someone won't trust you. It's like an insult, is what it is. "Nothing up my sleeves" is all you can say when you see them get that look. But sometimes if you mention your own children, that makes them think twice.

I have never in my life tricked anyone into buying an encyclopedia. Every one of my customers, I tell them that owning an encyclopedia isn't going to make them smarter. "Look at me," I told Mrs. Kidner. "I've been driving around for twenty years with a set in the boot of my car, and it hasn't rubbed off on me yet." Just spending the money isn't going to get your kids to college. But if they want to use it, it's there for them and it can be the most powerful tool in the world.

I told my boy that on the phone one Christmas—he asked me how work was going—and he told me I'd been reading my brochures too long. "It's Christmas, Dad," he said. "Take a day off."

•

I started out with an old hand called Teddy Daws when I first joined the company. Been at it since he was demobbed in '46, Ted had. Real knight of the road. Always get me to give him the once-over, he would. He'd put his hand on my arm before we went in, look me in the eye, and say, "Tom, is my snout clean, then?" And he'd tip his head back for me to have a look. Then he'd bare his teeth and make me check for any bits of food.

Bloody bonkers he was, but Ted was the best rep I ever saw, and one of the kindest lads you could hope to meet. Ted had the company car in those days — a Hillman Hunter — and he used to give me a lift to Beth's boardinghouse when we were courting. She was from the old country, near Sligo, seven years younger than me and finishing up at nursing school. We'd met at a tea dance organized by the London Irish Club.

"Snout?" Ted'd say before I got out of the car. "Teeth? All right, off you go, but wipe that silly grin off your face or she'll never trust you." Made me feel a proper pillock. Ted used to say courting was the hardest sale of your life, because you were selling yourself. "Course we're always doing that, in a manner of speaking, but this time the customer knows it too." Ted was best man at the wedding, and Beth made me promise he wouldn't try and sell to any of the guests. She was afraid he'd pull a card out of his pocket for the priest when he gave me the ring. As it was, they got on like a house on fire.

"Good turnout," Ted whispered as we waited for Beth to come down the aisle. I tried to ignore him. "Betcha haven't seen this many salesmen in a church, Father, since Jesus chucked 'em out of the temple."

"Perhaps I could learn a thing or two from you," the priest whispered back, "the way my congregations are declining." He shook his head.

"Best time to be in sales, is that," Ted told him. "When no one believes in anything anymore. Talk about your competitive advantage."

Teddy's big idea was that selling was just like an argument. "People are reasonable," he used to say. "No one invites you into their house and hears you out and then calls you a liar to your face. You wouldn't do that in an argument with your missus or the kids. It's like losing your temper. All it means is you've

lost. The only way to win is to come back with a better argument, and that's our job — always having the best argument. You
try and persuade the customers that they need the book, and if
they get into it with you, they'll try to persuade you that they
don't. But then if they lose, it's too late to say, 'No thanks. I don't
want it.' "

Of course, the surest way of winning is to believe in what
you're selling. That was Teddy's first rule: "Never sell something
you don't believe in."

"But what if you don't believe in something?" I asked him
once.

"You're not trying hard enough." He grinned. "If all else fails
you, just believe in belief."

●

Beth left me when Kevin was six, but things started going wrong
long before that. When she was expecting, she used to call me at
the office all the time. I had to start lying, saying I had another
call, just to get some work done. "You've got more time for your
customers than you have for me," she used to say. This was in
the early seventies. The country was in a shambles, sales were
down, and I was working a fifty- or sixty-hour week just to make
ends meet.

Then she phoned once and I was on a call and the reception-
ist didn't recognize her voice. "Can I transfer you to another
representative?" she asked, and Beth said, "Why not?" I got
home and she was grinning from ear to ear like it was some big
joke and there was Don, one of the lads from the office, with all
the brochures spread out and looking confused. Afterward Beth
said she was just interested in my work. It was natural, she said,

for a wife to be interested in what her husband did. I had to slip Don a couple of good tips to make up for the waste of his time, and I told Beth not to call me at the office anymore except in an emergency.

After Kevin was born, things were better for a while, except Beth kept at me to work less and spend more time at home. How could I, I told her, with things still tight at the office and an extra mouth to feed? That winter she began having salesmen visit her at the house every few days. Insurance blokes, double-glazing salesmen. "They're just so friendly and helpful," she'd say. I'd come in some evenings and hear Beth going, "There's my husband now." Then I'd have to watch some vacuum cleaner salesman sprinkle ash on my carpet or an insurance rep show us bright color slides of investment growth and life expectancy. Once it was even Mormons!

"That's very nice," I'd say, "but we're really not interested." It got where if I came home and saw a big shiny car in the drive, I just turned around. When I rolled in later, Beth would be in tears because some salesman couldn't wait for me to get home. "It's embarrassing, don't you see?" she'd say. "I kept telling him my husband would be home any minute."

Kevin, oddly enough, loved it. Beth said I didn't play with him enough, but he got lots of attention from the salesmen and they were always giving him glossy leaflets and free pens to play with. It got so bad at one point he had to ask me, "What do you sell, Dad?" "Meself," I told him wearily. I was taking one of those cheapo pens off him before he dropped it down the side of the sofa or let it leak on the upholstery. "Your old man sells himself." He didn't get it. "But *then* what do you sell?" he asked. "Afterward?"

Of course, I knew what was going on. Salesmen like to drop
by in the afternoon when the wives are at home. I've done it myself. There's always a little flirting, I suppose. We used to joke
about it round the office, but I never thought much about it myself until Beth started having all these fellas calling. I started
stopping by in the afternoon if I was on a call close to the house,
just to see if there was a car in the drive. It only happened the
once and she got rid of him sharpish — quite rude she was too, I
felt sorry for the bloke — but then she wanted me to stay for a
cuddle. When I told her I had to get back to work, she got angry.
"What did you come for, then?" she said.

In the end, I had to ask her. It was distracting me too much. I
asked her if any of the salesmen had ever tried it on with her.

"One or two," she said. "But they leave off when I tell them
my husband's a salesman too."

I nodded.

"Honor among thieves, is it?" she asked, all sarky.

She promised she'd stop inviting them in, but every so often
I'd come home and something would be funny. The upholstery
would smell different or the windows would look cleaner; all the
shoes would be lined up, shiny with polish, or the spots on the
curtains would have vanished. Beth would say nobody'd been
round.

"You're lying."

"You know, you're right," she said. "Now that I think about
it, the hoover rep dropped by, and we did it on the living room
carpet. He knows all about a good shag. Is that what you want
to hear?"

Another time she told me to ask Kevin if I didn't believe her.
He was playing nearby, turning the pages of a kid's book, even

though he was too young to read. But I said to leave him out of it.

"We've got to have trust," I told her.

"We'd need a lot less trust if you were ever here."

"What's that supposed to mean?"

"What about you?" she said. "What about you out every evening? What am I supposed to think?"

"It's completely different," I said. "It *happens* to be my job. I'm doing it for all of us."

"We could make do with less," she said, and I gave her a right rollicking then, called her a cow, told her she was throwing it all back in my face.

"Don't you come that with me," she shouted. "You love it. You know you do. You love it more than me and Kevin put together." I had to crack her one, just to make her shut up. She started to cry, but I told her I'd never in my life hit a woman before and it was her own damn fault.

•

They left while I was at work, of course. Just scarpered. I came home from another twelve-hour day and there wasn't even a note. I was so worried I couldn't concentrate at the office. It was like I couldn't see the point anymore. This went on for about ten days, mind you, and I didn't make a sale the whole time until I heard from her. The first thing she said was "I'm not coming back to you, so don't get started. I just want to know what you're prepared to do for your son."

I told her I'd do whatever was necessary. I started at nine the next morning and sold my first books before elevenses.

She'd gone back to her village near Sligo and moved in with her mother. I kept sending her checks and thinking the two of them'd come back one day, but Beth went on saying how the village was such a good place for Kevin to grow up. Maybe she was right. She used to call from the corner phone box, and behind her I could hear kids in the street, a bicycle bell, sometimes even cows.

It was awful at first, the empty house. I couldn't go into Kevin's room without bawling. But it got better once I knew they were okay. I wanted to do right by them, and once I got stuck in at work, it kept me so busy I didn't have time to be unhappy.

On the phone, Beth used to ask me if I missed her, and I'd say, "Yes," and when she'd say, "Honestly?" I'd say, "Of course." That was our problem, she always said. She could never be sure when I was telling the truth. "I know you think you are," she told me. "But it's a pitiful thing in a salesman."

She kept saying she'd come back if I got a new job, but I didn't see how we'd make ends meet. Sales was the only thing I was halfway decent at.

Only once did she tell me how romantic I'd been. "What did you expect from a salesman?" I said.

"Was that all it was?" she wanted to know. "Just salesmanship?"

"Salesmanship in the service of love," I said. "Salesmanship in a good cause."

•

If I didn't believe in education, I don't think I could do this job. Force myself on other people. Go into the homes of complete strangers and take up their time.

Of course, the trick, if there is a trick, is to make it like you're not a complete stranger. The idea is to get to know the customers and let them get to know you. I ask them about their kids, what lessons they like at school and which ones they have trouble with. Everyone loves talking about their kids, and if the kids are there I talk to them too. If you can sell to the kids, they'll do the rest of your job for you. You won't have to say another word about buying the books to the grownups. That's why I was sorry that Mrs. Kidner's daughter wasn't there that day.

I always ask the kids what they want to be when they grow up, and if they say a scientist or a doctor, I know I'm onto a winner. I turn straight to Volume X, "Vole to Zygote," page 581. There's this big color picture of a bunch of black kids in the jungle somewhere. They're all grinning away, standing around a table covered in what looks like pink spaghetti. Then I make them read the caption: "Children at a medical center in Namibia examining the worms that an hour before were inside them." The kids just die, and while the parents are laughing, I shake my head and tell them that my boy always loved that. "Oh, you have children," they say, as if it's a new idea to them, and I tell them all about Kevin.

I've always been good with the payments to Beth. She told me so herself. "You've been a good provider," she used to say. "That boy has never wanted for anything." All I asked in return was that she write to me about him and send me photos as often as possible. That way I could talk about him to my clients like anyone else. He always got high marks at school, and I was that proud of him when he got into college.

•

There was a time, I think, maybe six months after she left, that Beth might have come back. She said Kevin was unhappy. He wanted his dad. I didn't know what to say to that. It had been so long, the thought of it made me feel funny. I'd got used to my life, and I was selling better than ever, top of the table every month.

Beth put Kevin on the phone, and he asked me if we were all going to live together again. He didn't like all the Irish kids calling him a Brit, he said. He told me how much he missed me. Said what a great time we had on the weekends. I told him I needed to sort some things out with his mother. I did like having Kevin for weekends, don't get me wrong. I'd take a half-day Friday, drive up to Holyhead, and meet him off the ferry. I used to pretend he was a sailor — "Aye-aye, Cap'n" and all that — even if he did look a bit green around the gills. We'd get a B&B in Rhyl, spend the days on the beach if the weather was good, at the pictures or in the amusement arcades if it rained. We ate fish and chips every night. Got on famously.

But when Beth came back on the line, I told her I wasn't so sure.

"Then it's me," she said. "Since you and Kev are getting on so well."

I told her that wasn't it.

"What, then?" she said, and I was silent. I didn't know what to tell her. I could hear an ice cream van drive by the phone box playing its tune. I thought, *I could just fancy an ice cream*, and then I heard Kevin asking Beth for one and her telling him "Shh" and how it'd spoil his tea.

"Go on," I whispered to her. "Let him have one."

"Oh, all right," she said, and I heard him whoop and run off. I laughed, but when she spoke again her voice was icy.

"So tell me. When you're with him, those weekends, you think it's work, don't you? Like he's a customer. What is it you think you're selling him, exactly?"

I was silent.

"Well, it's a great routine. A great bit, a great line, a great *pitch*. He can't get enough of it. Except you don't want him to buy, do you? All you know is how to go on selling."

"It's not like that," I managed. The phone against my ear was hurting me, and I realized I was pressing it against my head.

"Well, if it isn't him, it is me, isn't it? What else?"

And that's when she asked me if there was someone else.

Just like that it was. Like a gift. I knew at once—I've never been so sure of anything in my life—I could get away with it. Those moments are so rare. When you know, you *know*, you're going to be believed, that someone trusts you. In sales, you live for moments like that. You can't turn your back on them.

"Yes," I said.

Done. Just like that.

Occasionally she would ask about this other woman I was supposed to be seeing, and I had to tell her something. Her name was Sarah, I said. She was divorced.

"Was she a customer?" Beth asked.

"That's right," I said. "A librarian."

It was easy. Beth didn't want to know much. She didn't ask, for instance, if I had been seeing Sarah before she left. I was relieved. I don't know what I would have told her. It was Kevin who wanted to know everything.

"Does she have kids?" he said. "How old is she?"

I thought for a minute. "No children," I said. "And she's thirty-six."

He kept on wanting to meet her.

"She's very busy," I told him.

"Doesn't she want to see me?"

"She's shy," I said.

Once or twice he asked me if I had a picture of her — "Someplace," I said — but after a while he stopped mentioning her. It felt bad lying to him, but it was for his own good. We still had great times together, and this way he got the very best of me. At any rate, a few months later Beth took up with some bloke called Conor, and that was that, really.

●

This is how bad a salesman I'd be if I were in any other line of business, anything other than encyclopedias.

I was out in Greece on holiday with Kevin one time. He would have been about thirteen then. We went down to the market. I asked him if he wanted to try on a leather jacket. He started grinning like the Cheshire Cat. I knew he'd been after one for ages, but his mother wouldn't get him one.

He wanted to buy the first one we saw, but I made him wait. "Look and you might learn something," I told him. We went from stall to stall looking at the prices they had marked, doing research, like. All the traders seemed to have the jacket he wanted for about a thousand drachmas, so I said to him, "We won't be too ambitious. We'll try and get one for eight hundred." We went around some more, looking for a likely-looking stall, and all the time I'm thinking, "Eight hundred, eight hundred, eight hundred." Then Kevin points out a little place with some good-looking jackets and he tries on a few, trying not to look too interested, just like I told him. We pretend to leave, and the little man stops me at the door and asks if we see anything we like, and I just point at the one Kevin fancies and go casually, "How much?"

And he says, "Eight hundred."

And I say, *"Done!"*

And Kevin says, *"Dad!"*

The funny thing is that afterward I went off thinking, "Damn, I could have had it for less," and I was really kicking myself. It was a boiling hot day, and Kevin wouldn't even carry the jacket. He said it smelled funny, and I snapped at him, and we had a scene. "I only got it for you," I told him. "Well, I don't want it," he shouted. "You're useless. I don't want anything from you." I remember there were these little kids following us around, spitting grape seeds at the backs of our legs, but we just ignored them and walked back to the hotel. He went to our room and wouldn't come out and I went down and sat by the pool on my own. I ordered a beer, but when it came I just put the glass against my head to cool down. It was our last day on holiday, and when we got back to England, he'd be going back to his mother.

I asked myself why I'd got so angry. I'd bought a nice jacket for about half the price I'd have paid in England, so why was I so upset? And I realized it was because I lost. The salesman beat me. That's what I was so angry about. And I didn't stop feeling angry until I thought how he must feel. He was probably sitting there thinking the same thing. He must have been telling himself, "What a fool I am. I could have said two thousand drachmas and that stupid tourist would have said yes." So we were both cursing ourselves, and for what? He'd still made a sale for a good price and I'd still got a jacket for a good price. It all equaled out. Everyone should have been happy!

That's why I'm grateful that they don't let us bargain on this job. When I sell something, there isn't a winner and a loser. Bargaining just makes people uncomfortable. Here I am trying to persuade you of something, of how much these books are worth, and if we end up haggling, it means that everything I've been saying to you is a lie. I think this is worth what it's worth and that's what I'm selling it for. When I told Mrs. Kidner that, she said, "Bravo!"

•

Kevin only told me he was dropping out of college because he wanted to come and stay with me while he looked for work in England. It was his mother's idea, he said. I got home from work one afternoon, the summer before last, and there he was, sitting on the sofa watching cricket with a can of beer in his hand. I'd given him a key, but it was so long since he'd come to see me that I assumed he had lost it. I was pleased that he had kept it safe all this time, but I couldn't understand why he was dropping out of college.

"I just am," he said. "Look. I've been over all this with Mum. Graduates aren't any more likely to get jobs now than anyone else, and I wasn't enjoying it, so why not start looking for something now? The sooner I start looking, the sooner I'll get something, right?"

I asked him if he was interested in anything in particular and he told me he wanted to get into advertising, "eventually." Said perhaps I'd inspired him. "All them samples, pens, brochures, and stuff you used to bring home when I was a kid—I loved that."

I wondered what he was planning to do in the meantime.

"Well," he said, "I know you contribute to my college expenses. I thought you wouldn't mind going on with that. After all, once I find a job, you won't need to help out any longer. You'll be saving in the long term."

I told him he was being an idiot. He might get some job now,

but how was he ever going to get on without a degree? I was paying for him to go to college, but he shouldn't expect me to pay
for this foolishness.

"But it's the same money," he said. "You'd have spent it
anyway."

"It's what I'm spending it on that counts."

"You're spending it on me either way," he shouted.

I told him not to talk to me like that. I told him I was his father, but he just laughed.

"You're unbelievable," he said. "Unbe-fucking-lievable."

I followed him around the house as he picked up his things
and went out the door. He wouldn't even let me give him a lift to
the station. Just walked up the road with his bags. I haven't seen
him since.

I keep calling Beth to ask her if she's heard from him, but she
says she hasn't.

"What did you say to him?" she asked the first time. "You
didn't raise your hand to him?" Now she just says she has no
news of Kevin, but I don't know if she's telling the truth or not.

"It'll blow over," she said once. "You'll see. It's not as if he
doesn't love you."

I told her I wasn't so sure.

"Oh, I forgot," she said. "You never would let anyone else
convince you of anything, would you? You always had to be the
one."

"Just let me know if he needs anything," I told her. "Anything
at all. I mean it."

"Oh, Tom. I know you do," she said softly. "If only sincerity
were enough."

•

Last month, when he found out about Mrs. Kidner, my boss called me in and wanted to know what I thought I was playing at.

"Couldn't you tell?" he said. "According to her son, the house is like a shrine to that little girl."

I told him it seemed perfectly normal to me.

"Well, we've got to cancel the order. The son says she does this from time to time. He doesn't mind people humoring her a bit, but he says he'll write to the papers if we put the sale through. It could be very embarrassing for the company."

"She wanted them," I said. "She really wanted them. I wouldn't have sold them to her if she didn't want them."

"But she doesn't need them. She's buying them for a dead girl. The company can't do that. It looks like we're taking advantage."

"She can afford it," I said. "I saw her house. I wouldn't sell to anyone who couldn't afford it. And she wanted them. Just because it's in our interests doesn't change that."

"I hope this isn't about your commission."

"Christ, no. What do you think I am?"

"Tom?" my boss said, more gently. "Tom?"

"Yes?" I said.

"What are you thinking of?" He came round his desk and stood in front of me. "What is going on in your head?"

"I don't know," I said. "I just don't see how it could hurt her."

That's when he first asked me about early retirement. "It's just an option. But maybe you should think about it."

Someone had to go round and pick up the books from Mrs. Kidner's house, of course. I didn't have to, but I asked if it could be me. My boss looked at me hard.

"I'd like to," I said.

"No monkey business, all right?"

"Come on," I said. "Give me some credit."

Before I rang the bell, I looked at myself in the mirror in the car. I blew my nose and looked again and then I went in to her. "Remember me?" I said when she opened the door.

She had the books all set up on built-in shelves in the little girl's room, and she watched me sullenly as I took them down one by one. I could only carry five volumes at a time, so it took a while. Afterward there was a strange blank space on the wall: just the empty bookcase, like a dark wooden box.

She didn't offer me a cup of tea this time, but at the door I said, "Look, I'm sorry. There's nothing I can do about it." She just looked through me. I wanted to tell her that I'd tried to let her keep them, that I'd got into hot water for her. I said, "My boy — what I told you about him — I lied. He won't even talk to me anymore."

She looked at me properly then. I wanted her to believe me so much.

"More fool you," she spat, and shut the door.

When I was rearranging the books in the boot of the car, I opened the first volume. The inscribed page was still there. I read it over to myself, and then I ripped it out and stuffed it in my pocket. I thought of Kevin and me, one night when he was just starting school, hunched over the kitchen table reading all about prisms and the refraction of light and how that made the sky blue. And then he asked me what happened when you died. I looked at Beth and she smiled crookedly, and I told him gently I didn't know, while the pages fluttered out from under my thumb.

I might have fought the retirement — I gave them my best years, after all — but the boss told me he had to let somebody go.

His hands were tied. Volume was down. The job was changing. "The only people going door-to-door nowadays are Jehovah's Witnesses, and they're giving the business a bad name," he said. If it wasn't me, it would be one of the younger lads. I was the wrong side of fifty-five, so it wouldn't affect me like some of them in their forties, with no chance of getting another job in this town, and some of them still with young kids.

And when he put it like that, I had to admit it made a sort of sense.

EVERYTHING YOU CAN REMEMBER IN THIRTY SECONDS IS YOURS TO KEEP

THE COURT HAD GIVEN ME six months to prove I was a responsible adult and a fit mother. "But how am I supposed to do that?" I wanted to know. "How am I supposed to prove I'm any kind of mother if they take Luke away?" "Catch-22," Billy said, like that explained it. Billy was no help. Luke was two months old and we were twentywhatever, but his eyes when they took him away seemed older than anything.

When we got home, Bill said he was sad. He said he was going out to score, did I want to come? But I just sat there on the sofa and shook my head. Luke was supposed to be a new start for us. I'd cleaned myself up when he was inside me, but when I came home Bill wanted to do some celebrating. "Yes!" He held Luke overhead like the Stanley Cup. "I'm a dad!" He rolled himself a joint as fat as a cigar and when he passed it to me he called me Mamacita and when I slid it back I called him Daddy-o. I'd been high on Luke when I was pregnant, but coming home all sore to our apartment in the converted motel on Ferry was a downer. I needed a little pick-me-up. I'd been clean as snow for nine months, but after all the Demerol and ephedrine they'd pumped into me during labor, I figured a few tokes wouldn't much matter. I crashed pretty quick, but then I woke up to Luke's crying.

Billy told me to lie back down: "Papa-san's got it covered." He was so proud, he was grinning like a cartoon of himself. I heard Luke yelling and Bill walking up and down with him, talking softly, telling him in a deep voice, "Luke, I *am* your father," and laughing to himself until he set the baby off again. I must have zoned out again. Sometime after that's when Billy got the idea to blow smoke in Luke's face to mellow him out. It worked fine, and Bill was smug as fuck in the morning. "It's the crying cure," he said. But Luke was still sleeping at lunchtime, and when I put my head close his breathing was bad, whistly like a slow flat, and I screamed at Bill until he took us to the hospital. Luke was okay then, but the nurse called social services on us.

Luke's toys were everywhere still, but I couldn't put them away yet. I hugged one of our old cushions to my stomach, stroked it. Ever since I was a kid I've had a habit of squeezing feather pillows until one of the little quills pokes through the fabric and I can tease it out. There are always little wisps of feathers on our rug. I was working on another one in the pillow now, pressing the sharp point against my finger until it punctured the cover, strumming it back and forth, finally plucking it out. This pillow used to be plump and soft; now it's skinny and no good for sitting. One corner was crusty from where Luke had sucked on it. You could still smell his diapers, even though the social worker had taken him away a week before. It made me think of the times I pressed my face to his belly when I changed him. He smelled *so* good. Like a fresh can of coffee or a new T-shirt, the kind of smell you can't get enough of in one breath. Sometimes I'd just run my nose all over him, sniffing him up while he giggled and squirmed. I wondered who'd look after him now. A foster mother, they told us. "A methadone mom," Bill said when the lawyer explained it, and that started me crying because it made me the stuff Luke was coming off. I tried to imagine her, this replacement mom, but all I could picture was my own mother. She was a fit mom. She was a responsible adult. And look how I ended up. Moms was all alone down there in Arizona living in one of those retirement communities where they do your cleaning and buy your groceries for you. I hadn't seen her since I ran off in '86, but I kept a P.O. box because she sent checks sometimes. I still had the letter she wrote me when Dad died and another when she moved from Texas four years ago. And then it struck me. Maybe she could come up here to Eugene and help us get our shit together. If she lived with us, maybe the court would change its mind.

Having Luke was so much pain, I thought I was being torn in two. I wasn't going to give him up now.

I thought of calling Moms up, but I hadn't done that for a long time, and if I did it now, with this news, it might not be so good. The shock might kill her, I thought. The shame, most likely. We should go see her, drive down there. Sure, I thought. Drive down there and get her.

I told Bill when he got back and he looked at me like, "Your mom?!"

"I do have one."

Jeez.

He didn't want to, but I told him we had to. He knew that look. He'd seen it before, when I was strung out. My gotta-score look. Besides, he loved road trips, popping speed. They made him feel like Hunter Thompson, even in our two-tone '87 Voyager.

It took us eighteen hours, and when we got there my back was aching but he was still wired. "Howdy," he said (he'd been talking like that since Flagstaff), giving Moms a big hug. "Howdy, ma'am." But then he couldn't sit still. He had to stretch his legs, he said, walking about bowlegged as if he'd gotten off a horse. That made her laugh. He was like a big kid. At least he broke the ice. But I couldn't watch him the whole time, and every so often he'd whistle and call out, "You've got some right purty stuff here. My, my." He was taking shit! I knew it. I wouldn't have minded, but that old family stuff was Luke's too now. "Whatever happened to that silver ashtray, Moms?" I asked her when I saw him come back with his pockets bulging. "And that nice table lighter?" But she couldn't remember. Then Bill said he had to go out, "get me some smokes." I followed him to the door and saw him throw another pill back, slapping his hand over his mouth with a little pop and dry swallowing, but when he saw me looking he made like an Indian brave, patting his hand over his mouth, making that woo-woo noise they make, and doing a rain dance down the hall. I told Moms he was shy, but she said he was sweet. I watched her carry the teacup she'd set for Bill to the kitchen, and it shook in its saucer as if she'd seen a ghost.

"Jesus, Moms," I said, "when d'you get so old?"

I guess she had me when she was thirty-eight or -nine already. For a long time they didn't think they could have kids, my folks, and then there I was. Now Moms's hair was white and thin and she walked with her head down, watching her feet. But she was pleased to see me, although it took her a minute to figure out who I was. It'd only been nine years, for Christ's sake.

So we sat around and chatted. We had some laughs. People dropped by. Friends of Moms's. She called them all up to tell them she had a visitor. "My daughter," she said proudly. She told them all I was in town on business and I thought she'd got it wrong, but then she winked at me and I said I was in . . .

"Computers." She was still sharp, Moms, I thought, and she could help me out with the court, I was sure of it. She looked like the perfect grandma, even if she didn't know she was one yet. It wasn't until later, after the friends had gone and we were alone, that I told her, and then she just sat there very still and I had to tell her again. "A little boy," I said. "Called Walt." Walter was my dad's name. I'd thought of this in the van on the way down. I'd been saving it up. And then I saw the tears gleaming in her eyes and we held each other for a long time. And then I told her that I'd wanted to bring the baby to see her, but that I was in a fix, that I needed her help, and she nodded and said, Yes, yes, yes, anything, of course. The thing is, she didn't remember what had gone on before—all the shit I pulled before. Just didn't remember it one bit. "Forgive and forget," she said. "That's my motto." I was so relieved. So long as she remembered who I was and that she was supposed to love me.

Bill called that night. He wasn't doing John Wayne anymore. The cops had picked him up. "Buying?" I said. "But you had a big stash." I'd seen him going into the trunk at rest stops every time I went to the bathroom. I thought he'd just packed for the trip. "Selling," he told me. I knew Billy dealt back in Eugene, but not out of the apartment, not around me since I kicked. If we'd been stopped carrying that kind of weight across state lines, we'd never have seen Luke again. Billy wanted me to bail him, so I said sure and hung up. "Who was that?" Moms wanted to know. I took a deep breath. "Just some sales guy," I said.

The thing about Bill is that I did love him, but then Luke came along and I *really* loved him. When Moms asked me what happened to my friend, "the cowboy," I told her he'd had to ride off into the sunset.

The next morning I got up early, took her coffee and told her to get packed. I went down to the condo office and told them she'd be staying with me for a while. The lady at the desk looked surprised. She asked me if I thought that was a good idea, and I said I thought it was a great idea.

On the road Moms was quiet the whole way. Kept looking at me and then out the window and then back at me, as if she thought I might turn into someone else. The radio was busted, so I tried to talk to her about the old days, the house, Dad, but she didn't say anything. I just started talking about whatever came into my head, like this old game show we used to watch. My dad was with Exxon then, and they wanted him in Scotland on account of the North Sea oil, so we were living in Aberdeen for a year. It was called *The Generation Game* — just a dumb show, with cheesy sets and bad toupées, really — and the gimmick was that the teams were dads and daughters, uncles and nieces, grandmas and grandsons. Happy families. There was a bit at the end, a memory test, where the contestants sat in front of a conveyor belt and watched all these prizes slide by, one by one. Then they got to sit in a spotlight and the host would tell them that everything they could remember in thirty seconds was theirs to keep. "Toaster," they'd go. "Blender, golf shoes, cuddly toy." There was always a cuddly toy. But then they'd start to forget things and the audience would go nuts, calling out, "TV, tennis rackets, mixer." And the host would be shouting, "You've got that already. What else, what else?" By the end of it some of the contestants could barely remember their own names. The prizes weren't much and it was real corny, but we loved it, yelling at the TV, screaming at them what they forgot.

"That'll be us," I told Moms. "You and me, playing the Generation Game."

We were close that year, two Americans in Scotland. We went

to all the castles together. I couldn't understand the accents of anyone at school and all they knew about Texas and oil was *Dallas*. For the first time, Moms and I had more in common than anyone else we knew. But that was also the year I started getting high. On gas fumes first—a *fuck you* to my dad the workaholic oil man—then later sniffing glue, doing whip-its behind the cafeteria. It felt so dumb passing around a tube of glue; it was just a game. But then when we moved back to Houston, I got serious. Dope, coke, crack, smack. Moms was playing her own games back then: moving the cocktail hour up from five to four to three to two, the vodka greasy, straight from the freezer; watching the soaps all afternoon. But finally she sobered up long enough to tell me I had to choose: my home or my habit; her or the heroin. It was no choice at sixteen. Not even close. I kept in touch with Dad for a few years after I left. He would meet me for coffee, take me for a big dinner, or if I was too fucked buy me sacks of groceries (always frozen dinners: chicken cordon bleu, Salisbury steak, stuffed peppers—like I was too busy to make my own). He gave me money too, though he always made me promise not to spend it on shit. He told me that after I left, she just stayed in her room for weeks, hugging herself. She never went out, didn't eat, just lay there in the dimness with the drapes closed. And she was drinking, working her way through years of accumulated duty-free—Cuervo Gold, Curaçao, Kahlua.

"She won't even answer the phone," he said, meaning in case it was me.

"I'm not as strong as her," he said, meaning he still had to see me, behind her back.

He was still hooked, I told him, but she was going cold turkey. Meaning from me. In her first letter to me, when she told me he was gone—heart attack in the yard—she said he'd made her promise to do what she could for me. I took the money she sent, but I knew enough not to get in touch. She didn't need me back in her life. Not after she'd kicked me. And yet here I was again.

Outside, the road was rough; it sounded like static under the tires until we hit one of those patches of fresh tarmac, when everything went quiet for a moment. It was like trying to tune a radio, except all I could hear in the good spots was Moms breathing.

We stayed at a Snooz Inn just outside Salt Lake (I put it on Moms's Visa), shared a room for the first time in twenty years. When she came out of the bathroom to go to sleep, she had her head caught in her nightgown and I had to get up and help her set it straight, but then when her head appeared she was all flustered. "I can manage," she said, and then I felt embarrassed in just my bra and panties, stretch marks and tracks still showing.

It was raining when we got to Eugene, which saved me from giving Moms the tour. I wouldn't have known what to say anyway. Billy always liked to call it "the town where the sixties never died." He liked to say he came to college here on account of Ken Kesey—that and the fact they filmed *Animal House* down the block—and stayed because Springfield was the crystal-meth capital of the West.

When we got to our apartment it was dark, which I thought would help, because the building looks better at night, although sometimes the johns from Seventh like to cruise you. She just took one look and said "Well!" and rolled her sleeves up and went right at it. She found all that crap under the sink—Windex, Mr. Clean—from the last tenants, and I cut up an old maternity dress for a rag, but when I tried to help she just waved me away, so I left her to it, fetched her stuff from the van, and made up a bed for myself on the Goodwill sofa. She was happy, I thought. Humming! Happy to be doing, to be needed, I guess. But just when she was going great I heard her give a little cry. She was in the kitchen, and when I went in, it seemed so beautiful. It shone. She was mopping, there was water on the floor, but then I saw she was wet. "An accident," she said in a strangled voice, and I could tell she wanted to run to the bathroom, she kept lifting her feet, but she couldn't because she didn't want to get pee everywhere, and she was whimpering with the frustration. Well, I helped her out, of course. The mess wasn't much compared to shooting galleries I've seen, though I didn't tell her that. Got her changed—turns out there was a pack of diapers, big ones, in her case, but she'd forgotten to put one on—threw her dress in the sink, and cleaned up. "You cleaned up after *me*," I told her through the bathroom door. "What goes around comes around."

And that's how we went at it those first few weeks. Me looking after her, and her cooking and cleaning and looking after me. I had a lot of trouble with the breast pump. It hurt and I didn't like to use it, but then my breasts would leak all over. The smell of my milk always made me cry for Luke. But Moms helped me with the pump, boiling up the plastic pieces in a saucepan on the stove before I used it. She wiped my breasts, caught a drop on the end of her finger and tasted it. "That's good stuff," she said, and she held out her finger to me and I licked it. She made me get little bottles to sterilize and store the milk in, and we kept a stash of them in the fridge to supply the social worker when I saw her each week. Luke didn't like formula, she told me, and it made me glad to think of him still jonesing for me.

Moms could look after me and the house like in the old days, but looking after herself, that's where I came in. She had trouble keeping the order of things straight. She kept flushing before she went to the bathroom and forgetting to after, and once I found her rolling deodorant on after she'd put on her blouse. The shower was tricky for her too, until we got her a plastic lawn chair in there, and afterward I'd help dry her off, dust her with talc, and work in the lotion. At night I rubbed her back and her legs and feet. Her legs were knotted with veins, the muscles hard like wood, but I liked to rub on them until they loosened up and she purred with pleasure. Then, before bed, I combed her hair out till it crackled and shone.

The only problem with all this cleaning was I could no longer smell Luke anywhere. I put a onesie of his on a stuffed chimp and slept with it, but soon it just smelled like me. At night I kept waking up thinking I heard him, but it was only the whining of neighborhood dogs or the hooting and bleating of trains in the yards over by Fifth. Those were the nights I wanted something bad, when I remembered how good it was getting high. Once I got up, started going through the cupboards, thinking Bill must have one last stash. But then I heard Moms moving around. I thought she was on the way to the bathroom. "Can't sleep, sweetheart?" She was at the door, her face dark beneath her white hair, like a negative of herself. She was holding out her hand. So I went with her, curled up beside her in bed. I still woke up, but it wasn't so bad as alone.

The apartment was looking in great shape when the social worker, Ms. Ross, came to visit. I'd first met her before at the courthouse. She'd asked me to step outside to talk so she could smoke. She told me how it would go, and when we were done she stubbed out the butt before it was half gone. "Trying to quit," she told me. "Good luck," I said, and she blushed.

Now she looked around at the tidy living room, the swept floors, and she seemed surprised. She asked about Bill and I said he'd split, that I'd told him to go. "If you're not part of the solution . . . ," I told her firmly. "So you're a single mom," she said, making a note in her book. "How d'you feel about raising a child alone?" Which was perfect really, because I got to go, "I'd like you to meet someone." It was like unveiling a statue. I'd told Moms to dress nice and wait in the bedroom until I called her, and now she came out, and her makeup that I'd only helped her with a little was great and she had on a tweedy suit and her pearls, only she still had her hair in rollers. I didn't know what to say, but the social worker didn't seem to notice. Moms just came on in and said hello, pleased to meet you, and sat herself down. I tucked an afghan around her and we went on just as happy as you please. Afterward Moms and I laughed about it. I took out her curlers and she patted her hair in the mirror and we both agreed it had come out fine.

When the social worker left, she told me she was pleased with my progress. She said she could see that family was important to me, and then she got back in her Saturn. When she waved, I saw that under her sleeve she was wearing a nicotine patch. I went in and gave Moms a hug, and she beamed like Mr. Clean. We had visits then every two weeks, and they went well. On the second visit Luke was allowed to come and play for a while. I fed him while Moms and the social worker (her name was Carrie) watched and chatted. He was so greedy it made me laugh. The social worker kept talking about Luke—Luke this, Luke that— and Moms kept saying how Walt was a great baby too, until I explained that his name was Walter Luke. Carrie looked at her paperwork again and then at me and I said, "Yes," and nodded at her and I saw her write it down. When Walt pooped I got out the baby works and changed him. His diapers seemed so small compared to Moms's, his skin, as I ran the wipe over it, so soft. Afterward I just held him and held him, and it was like the best fix in the world. When I gave him up at the end of the day, I was sweating, shaking, and Moms held me and told me, "Oh, darling, I know, I know."

About a week later Bill showed up at the door. He'd left a few messages on Moms's machine back in Phoenix that I'd listened to and erased, but I'd been half expecting him. I guess he got a bail bondsman to get him out, but I was pretty sure he was breaking some law or other coming all the way to Oregon like that. I was in the bathroom, but I heard his voice at the door when Moms opened. She was very nice to him, but she made like she didn't know who the hell he was. Bill just stood there and whined about this being his place and Moms told him quietly that it couldn't be and he couldn't come in and then she started shouting "Rape!" in her little-old-lady voice and Bill just beat it after that. The last I heard of him was his footsteps twanging down the metal stairs outside. He took the van, which was his anyway, but I figured that was worth it to see the back of him. Besides, he probably lost it to the bondsman anyway, when I called in a tip that he'd left the state. He was a tattooist, Bill, so I knew he'd do okay inside. Sometimes after a sitz bath I'd look at the little lizard he did on my shoulder and I'd think, *You were an artist, Bill, as well as an asshole.* Moms and I laughed over it all night, and she kept it up the whole time, saying she'd never seen him before in her life. "Come on!" I said.

At the next visit, Carrie asked me to bring Walt down to the car with her. It had been a great visit. Moms had been playing with Walt, peekaboo and that, and when I said it was time for the baby to go, she held him for a second, kissed his head, gripping his hair in her teeth for a second. "He smells just like you did," she told me, handing him over. "Takes me back."

In the lot, Carrie complimented me on the apartment, on turning my life around. "I admire the way you care for your mother," she said. I just beamed at her. "I would like to recommend that Walt be returned to you," she said, and I thought my smile would just break my mouth.

"Thank you," I said, but quietly, because the baby was sleeping. "Thank you. Thank you. Thank you."

But Carrie shook her head. "I'd like to," she said. "You've proved yourself a responsible caregiver. You'd be a good mother. But I'm not sure the circumstances in your home are ideal for a child."

"What do you mean?" I hissed. "Isn't it clean enough?"

"I mean your mother," she said. "She's trying her best, but she shows several marked symptoms of Alzheimer's. I'm concerned she represents a potential danger to herself and to the baby. While you and Walt were playing I saw her get up to make coffee, put the kettle on the stove, and turn the gas on, but forget to light it. I had to turn it off myself. She leaves cleaning supplies in easy reach of the child, despite my reminders. She's called the baby by your name at least twice in my hearing. Last visit I saw her put a foil package in the microwave."

"Oh, that microwave hasn't worked for weeks," I told her, but she just nodded, and I wanted to bite my tongue. What I didn't tell her was that the milk in the coffee Moms made the last visit had been mine, near as I could figure.

"I have an older parent myself. I don't know if I could do what you're doing. I'm sympathetic, really. But it's my duty to put Walt first. Can you tell me you can watch him and your Mom twenty-four hours a day?"

"Yes! Sure!"

She shook her head.

"So what you're saying is it's okay for me to be a single mom, just not a single daughter?"

She just put a piece of nicorette gum in her mouth and chewed.

"Well, what am I supposed to do?"

She looked at me. "I can't tell you that," she said, holding out her hands for the baby.

I stood in the parking lot for a long time after she left. It was October, and it was starting to get dark earlier. The sky was gray, a sheet of high cloud cover with dirty little clouds below it. I watched a mother walk by with an empty stroller and a kid a little older than Walt walking along beside, pushing a toy stroller with a doll in it.

When I went back, I looked at Moms. She was at the sink washing the mugs, even the empty coffee can. She always saved them. You never know when you might need something. When she saw me watching, she dried the suds off her hands, still red from the water, and smiled. "I like your friend Carrie. What a lovely baby she's got."

•

I took the bus with Moms back to Phoenix the next week. Her friends were pleased to see her. "Everyone's so friendly here," she said, beaming. She marched around the room like it was a hotel or something. She ran her fingers over the shelves looking for dust. Finally she said, "I'll take it."

"I'll visit," I told her. "With Walt." She nodded.

"You're the best, Moms," I told her, and she said, "Not hardly. Look at the mess I made with you."

That made me jump, but then I saw she was joking.

"No," she said. "You make me proud."

I'd waited all my life to hear her say it, and when she said it I knew she meant it, and she was wrong. Don't you remember? I wanted to yell. Don't you remember what I was like? The dope? The coke? The crack? The smack? The cuddly fucking toy!

Her forgetting it just made me remember it more.

I started crying then, but she told me, "Shh, shh, shh."

"I like it here," she said. She hugged herself and looked out the window. "You can see the world go by." I stood with her and watched a bunch of kids slide by on Roller Blades. Moms waved a little. I thought they'd give her the finger, but they didn't see her. A line of cars turned the corner, the sun flaring off the windshields one by one, like flashbulbs. "I like it here," she said again, closing the drapes a ways.

Later, on the street outside, I looked back up at her room and I waved. I couldn't see her; that desert sun was shining on the glass. I hoped she wasn't there, but I thought maybe she was. I got on the crosstown bus and rode down the street with my arm out the window the whole way, and then we took the corner. I thought of her at her window, dazzled by the light, turning around, her arm gone sore from waving, her eyes adjusting to the dimness of the room.

ON THE TERRACES

Y BROTHER LIES in a Midlands hospital dying of AIDS and I can't think of a single thing to say to him. I sit by his bed reading a newspaper while he sleeps, carefully turning the pages. Every few minutes I try to look up to see if he's awake. I watch the circles of condensation bloom and fade against his oxygen mask, and then go back to my paper.

My mother knits when she's here. A warm sweater for me, she says, holding up the pieces, pressing them against me. She smoothes the wool over my chest or shoulders and tells me I don't look after myself. She goes on knitting even if my brother's awake, and the snipping of the needles fills the silence between them when he's too tired to speak and she can't say a word without crying.

She calls her crying "waterworks."

I take her home each night at ten or eleven and we have a cup of tea together. I put a hot water bottle in her bed and leave her in front of the TV before I drive back to the ward. She can't go to sleep straight after seeing him, and often I come back in the morning and find her snoring softly on the sofa. She thinks one of us should always be at his bedside when my brother wakes. She wants us to make the most of his last conscious hours, and when the crisis comes she doesn't want to rely on the nurses to phone us in time. This shift system was the only way I could make sure she got any sleep.

By the time I get back to the hospital the next day's newspapers are piled in bundles in front of the small newsagent's kiosk in the lobby, and I buy two or three of them — *Times, Telegraph, Guardian* perhaps. I've been doing this for a week now, but it's still strange to see tomorrow's news on the front pages so late at night. Events seem to float free, as if they could happen as easily today as tomorrow or the next day.

On my brother's ward, the night nurses know me now, and we exchange whispered good mornings in the dead of night.

I've taken two weeks of annual leave to be here, and my brother feels bad about that. He tells me I don't have to stay. But I don't mind it at the hospital. It's peaceful, and I can't remember the last time I had the chance to read a newspaper from cover to cover. It wouldn't bother me if my brother slept right through the night, but usually he wakes every couple of hours, sometimes for a minute or two, sometimes for much longer. The medication makes him drowsy and has messed up his sleep rhythms.

He wakes blinking from a doze, but if he's been sleeping heavily he kicks his legs, swimming back to consciousness. He might go on like this for a minute or two, and I put my paper away and watch him until he wakes or falls back to sleep. His body makes only a slight ripple under the blanket when he's still. The bed looks unmade, as if someone had just slipped out for a moment, closed the covers to keep the warmth in, but left those thin rumpled folds. A sharp tug from one of his brisk nurses would make it all neat.

The problem is we've already said all the things we should say.

Last week when I came down he'd been rushed into hospital and they didn't think he'd make it. In the few hours after he regained consciousness, he made me go over the arrangements with him. I told him not to worry about our mother. He told me he loved me and I told him I loved him too, and at that moment — after not seeing each other or even talking on the phone for maybe three years — I think we actually meant it. At least we both wished we did. Since then the crisis has passed and he's stronger now, though not out of danger. For a few days we just repeated things we'd already said until we began to sound insincere, and since then we've had nothing to say to each other. I think we're afraid. Things are better between us now than for a long time, and we're afraid we'll say something to spoil it.

Tonight I look up and see he's awake. I've become engrossed in my paper — something about Thatcher and Europe — and I feel a sudden flush of guilt, caught out, more interested in the world than in him. But he's not watching me. He's reading the back of the paper, the headlines, the sports news. I hold the pages very still and watch his eyes move. When he's done with what he's reading, he looks at me and I say gently, "How're you feeling?"

"Bored," he says.

And then he asks me to tape the football match the next day and bring in our mother's TV and VCR tomorrow night.

"Will you do that for me?"

"Okay," I say, a little dubiously, not sure if I've been insulted, if he's bored by me.

"Only don't watch it," he says. "Don't listen to the score. I'm not watching it with you if you know how it ends."

•

The first time I ever saw my brother in a hospital was when he was eight and I was five. He'd had his tonsils out and he wasn't allowed to eat anything but ice cream. "The doctor said so," he told my mother. I was speechless. I thought he meant forever. I thought he meant he got to eat nothing but ice cream for the rest of his life. A bowl came while we sat there and we watched him eat it. Each time he took a mouthful he twisted the spoon before withdrawing it, licking it clean. It slipped slowly between his lips, like a bright steel tongue.

On the way home my mother bought me a block of Neapolitan ice cream — stripes of strawberry, vanilla, and chocolate like a flag. My father had left us about a year before, and all she cared about anymore was that the three of us got along.

The second time, my brother must have been fourteen. He'd broken his leg. My mother sat beside him at the head of the bed and I sat on the other side by his foot with a felt-tip in my hand. I looked at the huge looming cast and studied the strings and pulleys that held it up. I couldn't think of anything to write on all that whiteness. Later, after the other kids on the ward had come and scribbled on it and the plaster had gone gray with dirt at the edges and picked up fluff, I could have done it, but then, when it seemed so bright and perfect, I had no idea what to write. I had carved graffiti on desks at school with my compass point. Once Jase Johnson and I had drawn an arrow above the urinals. "Follow me," the arrow said. "Not much further now." Jase had had to get on my back with me grabbing his legs to stop him sliding off to write the last bit, right in the corner where the ceiling and the wall met, a sign saying, "You're pissing on your shoes."

But I couldn't think what to write on my brother's cast.

"Time to go," my mother said.

"Just a sec."

She said she'd meet me down the hall. She wanted to talk to the doctor.

When she'd gone my brother said, "I didn't tell."

He meant he hadn't told anyone that I had pushed him off the low brick wall at the end of our drive when he'd broken his leg. At school, in the toilets, I'd seen his name in a line of graffiti. Just his last name. I thought it meant me for a moment, and then I realized it meant him.

I didn't say anything. I stared at his cast thoughtfully and sucked my pen.

"It'll be our secret," he said.

I stooped down and pretended to scribble something on the base of his foot.

"What's it say?" he said. "What's it say?" But I just ran off.

•

I leave him at eight or nine each morning and drive home to pick up my mother. I roll my newspapers into a tight tube, and when I set them down on the kitchen table they slowly unclench. We have breakfast together, and then I drop her at the hospital and come home to sleep. My room hasn't changed since I left for college — the same movie posters on the wall, the same clothes in the drawers. I can't sleep in it, it feels too small, and often in the afternoon I get up, pull on my old, short robe, and look in my brother's room. His is the same, unchanged, with pictures of footballers all over the walls. He took them down when he came home a few months ago but didn't put anything up to replace them, and after he went into hospital this time my mother put them all back. They'd been up so long that the wallpaper had faded around them, and she just had to match the posters to the gaps. I walk around his room now, hands behind my back, peering at them, not wanting to touch anything. He never let me in here when we were kids. If he caught me, he'd push my face against the wall and twist my arm back until tears came to my eyes.

When he was fifteen he used to catch the train to London every fortnight to go and see a game. This would have been in the mid-seventies. He wore flared jeans and a denim jacket and a silky team scarf thin enough to keep folded in his pocket until he got near the ground. Once he showed me the Stanley knife he'd taken from our father's old toolbox. He slid the blade in and out and told me if he ever had to use it he'd go for the chin or the cheek. Autographing, he called it. The hooliganism was just getting bad then, but he told our mother he knew how to look after himself. He only pulled his scarf out when he found a crowd of home fans, and he peeled it off again whenever he was on his own. My mother said I could go if he took me, but he always refused, and when I was old enough to go myself I went to the movies instead.

I stand at the window and look out at the street for a moment and then draw the curtains and get into his bed.

I followed him once. As far as King's Cross station. It was odd seeing him there, the only person I knew in such a large crowd. It was hard not to call out, to run up and surprise him. He walked under the departure board and went into the gents', and I waited in a newsagent's looking at comics. I started to smile, thinking he'd been caught short. But he'd not come out after fifteen minutes. I thought he'd given me the slip, or he was waiting

in there for me. Men came and went, and every time I heard
steps I prayed it was him. It was as if he'd vanished. I waited another twenty minutes, panicky with impatience, too scared to go
in after him. In the end, I just left.

•

He is awake and in pain when I come to pick my mother up
the next evening. She tells me he's been refusing his medication,
and I can see that she's upset. He didn't think I'd wake him if he
was asleep. "Of course not for a stupid football match," my
mother says.

When I told her about taping the game earlier, she didn't
know what to make of it. I could tell she disapproved, but she
couldn't say why. All she made me do was check that it was okay
with the hospital, but when I told her that the nurse had said it
was a wonderful idea, she pursed her lips with disappointment.

"It's what he wants," I told her when I had her home and settled on the sofa. "I didn't think I could say no."

"Tell me," she said, "did you know? When the two of you
were young?"

"No." I was bent over the dark TV, one arm behind it feeling
for the cables. I watched her reflection in the screen. We've had
this conversation before, but this time something about her dis-
approval made me add, "I might have suspected."

"And you never thought to tell me?"

"I didn't know for certain."

"You should have told me anyway. I'm not saying I'd have
done anything different. But I'd have wanted to know."

"It wouldn't have changed anything."

"I would have known him better."

"Well," I said, "he hasn't always been that easy to know, has he?"

"You could talk to him," she said. "And not watch that rubbish."

I unplugged the TV and the VCR and carried them out one at a time to the car. When I came in to say I was going, she was still sitting on the sofa staring at the space where the TV had been. The whole room looked empty, all the chairs facing in at nothing. "Go on," she said.

At the hospital my brother watches me as I struggle in with the TV and the VCR. I balance them on separate plastic chairs and fiddle with the cables.

"You don't know the score, right?"

I shake my head.

"I'll know if you're lying."

"I don't know the score," I tell him, and he says, "All right, then."

After a minute he says, "How is she?"

"She'll be fine. How are you doing?"

"Just put the game on," he says.

Sometimes I want to shake the IV stand next to his head.

I press *play* and the screen fills with snow. I have one sickening moment of doubt, thinking that I've taped the wrong thing or brought the wrong tape, but then the screen fills with the bright green of the floodlit pitch.

My brother makes me turn up the volume until the commentary makes conversation impossible and the crowd noise fills the room. He has trouble hearing over the sound of his breathing. A male nurse comes to the door, attracted by the sound. He smiles and leans on the door frame and calls, "Didn't they play earlier?"

My brother ignores him. I nod and pray he won't give the score away. He smiles and pulls the door shut after him.

We are silent for a few minutes, and then, responding to the game, my brother says, "Shot," and I find myself nodding.

•

I've only asked him about his sex life once. It was a Christmas Eve about ten years ago, and we'd escaped a house full of relatives for the pub. It was heaving. We were only going to have a pint, but it took us so long to fight our way to the bar we ended up ordering doubles of whiskey too. We found a place to stand by the cigarette machine, a glass in each hand. I bent my head close to his and told him I was interested—"Not in who does what to whom or anything like that. Just how you live your life." I had the earnest intensity of someone on the verge of drunkenness, and he must have been in a similar state, or just carried away by the heightened holiday mood. He told me about "cottages," the public toilets where he met and had sex with men, sometimes two or three a night.

"Two or three a *night?*" I was dubious. "These are total strangers?"

He nodded.

"What do you say to them?" I was talking too loudly, and I sensed heads turning toward us.

"I don't *say* anything," he whispered. "I look them in the eye. I smile. There's a shared assumption. You don't need to talk about it."

It made me feel oddly unmanned. I leaned in, my arms encircling him, holding my drinks clear. I told him I couldn't sleep with women like that, even if they were available.

"Me neither," he said. I smiled, but he didn't mean it as a joke. "You can't compare them. It's not that I fancy men and you fancy women. It's about wanting the same or different. The sameness is what makes it all right."

No, I told him, I couldn't understand it, I didn't have a clue what he was talking about. He took a step back and shrugged and said it wasn't his idea to talk about it. I asked him why he couldn't just have one lover "like everyone else" and he said, "I don't want to talk about it anymore." He took a long sip of his beer and looked away over the rim of his glass.

I've done a lot of reading since my brother's diagnosis. I know how the pneumonia is filling his lungs. Spreading until he has no room to breathe. Crowding him out. But at another level, I realize, I have no idea why my brother is dying, what he's dying for.

•

At halftime I turn the volume down and offer to fast-forward through the commercials and the analysis.

"Are you in a hurry?" he says. He asks me if I watch a lot of football and I say, "Now and then."

"Are you having a good time?"

"Sure."

He is silent for a moment.

"I'm glad you're here," he says at last. "I can't stand watching a game alone, especially a taped one. It feels sort of pointless, like you're wasting your time. It's easier to pretend it's live if there's two of you."

"I usually watch on my own," I admit.

"It's not the same," he says. "You need a crowd, even if it's only two." I look over at him, but he's staring at the screen, not me, and I look back at it. "When I used to go to games, you'd be jammed in so tight you couldn't raise your arms. You all had to breathe together."

"It sounds dangerous," I say, but he shakes his head slowly, turning it on the pillow so that I can hear his hair rubbing against it.

"Warmest I've ever been in my life," he says. "They used to say it could rain cats and dogs on the terraces and your feet'd never get wet. When someone scored, I used to lift my legs and be carried twenty, thirty yards on this wave of men."

"I've never been. Not to a live game."

"You should. Once. Before they rip 'em all out."

He means the terraces. Since the disaster at Hillsborough, when all those fans died, the government has decided that the terraces should be replaced by seats.

It pleases me that my brother likes football. I used to think that he'd only pretended to be a fan, only gone along with it to fool us. After I knew he was gay, knew for sure, it was tempting to doubt everything I had known about him before.

"Tell me something," I say. "Why did you keep doing it?" He knows what I mean.

"Where do you want me to start?" There's an impatience in his voice. "What do you want to know?"

I must hunch my shoulders, flinch somehow, because all he says is "I don't know. It was freezing down there. Bloody fucking freezing."

•

The second half begins. After a few minutes he says, "Thanks for doing this."

"No problem."

"Really," he says softly, and then, "I'm going to sleep now." The way he says it makes it sound as though he has no choice.

"Should I switch this off?"

"No. You've got to tell me how it turns out."

I watch the rest of the game. I turn the volume right down until the players float soundlessly over the turf and the fans shout silent clouds into the cold night air. My brother's breathing settles, gets shallow and ragged, then settles again when I'm just about to call a nurse. The game ends in a draw and I unhook the cables, turn everything off, and sit with him for a while after carrying the TV and VCR out to the car. I've a new paper, and I open it slowly.

I've often thought about what he told me that Christmas. I still don't understand it. I imagine him down in one of those old Victorian WCs, tiled and echoing. I think of the casualness of it, the anonymity, the giving and the holding back. The silent understanding. It seems oddly familiar. There's a surprising maleness to it.

When I was thirteen I had a dark line of down along my upper lip, what we used to call bum fluff. My mother wouldn't let me shave. I was the clumsy one, and she was afraid I'd take my nose off or something. Instead she got my brother to do it. He grinned. This was about two years after I'd broken his leg. We'd never talked about it again. He carried one of the high kitchen stools into the bathroom, put a new blade in his razor, and tied a towel tightly round my neck, "to soak up the blood." He rubbed a handful of shaving cream over my face as if it were a custard pie, filling my ears, covering my mouth. He ran his fingertip lightly across my lips to uncover them. The blade scraped against my skin and pulled at the fine hairs, but I didn't say anything. He was very close, leaning over me, silent except for his breathing. He was concentrating hard, but he must have met my eyes once, because he said, "Don't look so worried. I won't cut you." When he was done, while I washed my face, he told me shaving would make my beard come in faster. The water felt like oil on my skin. "It's so smooth." I looked in the mirror, touching my face, and he stood behind me, grinning. I smiled back, but when I looked at my face again a tiny globe of blood was just beginning to swell at the corner of my mouth.

•

My mother is getting breakfast ready when I get home, and she asks me how he is and I say fine.

"What did you talk about?" she says, and I tell her, "Football." It's so ludicrous, I whisper it.

She looks at me, and for a moment I think she's going to say, "Men!" but all she says is "You don't even like football," and I shrug.

•

The local team are at home in February. The ground is at the end of an old residential street, the brick walls rising over the houses, the floodlights above them. I stoop in the darkness of the narrow turnstile and pass my money across to the ticket taker behind his grille and say, "One." He is so close I can smell the damp wool of his coat.

I lean on the turnstile and it gives slowly, depositing me in a dank brick tunnel, gently sloping, leading up to a broader concrete passageway. I can see the curve of the stadium for the first time in the distance. Banks of steps lead up to the left, and I take them quickly into the daylight. After the darkness, the smell of the brick, the closeness of the walls, the pitch is a revelation. The dull day seems bright; the muddy pitch glows green. It makes me wonder if this isn't the point, if the Victorian architects who built this place hadn't meant for all the darkness and dampness to lead up to this moment.

It's only a moment, though. It's a biting day, and I stand on the open terraces cowering in the wind. My brother died two months ago. I'm home for the weekend, as I have been for every weekend since. I want to see what he saw in something, but there are only two or three dozen men around me, gathered in little knots and huddles, stamping their feet on the bare, cracked concrete. We keep a wary, respectful distance. The stands with their plastic seats and bright red corrugated roofs look more modern, but this part of the stadium must be prewar. Shallow slabs slope down to the field, broken up here and there by chest-high iron stanchions. I cross my arms and lean my elbows on one of them, waiting for the game to begin.

Opposite, at the far end of the stadium, they've already begun the demolition. The home terraces will be rebuilt over the summer, but the away end is already half gone. Last night I read in the local paper that the contractors are working flat out, even during games. The club has erected a tall hoarding to hide the work from the pitch, and lads on a youth training scheme have painted it to look like a crowd scene. I can't make out any faces from so far away, but there was a photograph of it in the paper. Men with their mouths open, men with their hands in the air. The only sound coming from them is the ring of scaffolding going up and the thump of pneumatic drills. A local lady councillor has complained that there are four hundred and sixty-three figures in the crowd and not a single woman.

The home team are terrible, heavy-legged in the mud like cart horses. "Wankers," someone on the terrace shouts. At halftime boys with their hands stuffed in the pockets of dirty jeans come out and wander around the pitch stamping down divots.

The players run out again and the floodlights come on, although it's only four o'clock. The home team attack the goal in front of the terrace. They win a corner and have a shot fly just over the bar. It rises over the fence and lands among us. The men around me chase after it, running stiffly with their hands in their pockets. The ball skids across the concrete, bounces up off the edge of a step. One of them gets close enough to swing at it, but he misses and it bobbles down toward me. I think about letting it roll past but as it comes level stoop and catch it. The men running toward me stop. I hold the ball for a long moment, feeling the slight tackiness of the damp leather. Then I throw it out in front of me and swing, catching it on the full so that it sails over the fence. It's caught by one of the gusts of wind trapped in the stadium, and for a moment it hangs in the night, shining in the floodlights.

Somewhere in the crowd a thin cheer goes up, and behind me someone calls, "Shot!" I feel their eyes on me and I stand very still, not looking round while the sensation of striking the ball, the sweetness of the contact, slowly passes.

CAKES OF BABY

AT THANKSGIVING, Laura makes three pies for her mother—apple cinnamon, lemon meringue, and pumpkin. Her husband, Sam, watches her slide them gently one by one onto the back seat of their '88 Accord. She hems them in with coats and props a bag in front so they won't slide forward.

"You want to buy car seats for them?" Sam asks.

"You have to have pies at Thanksgiving," Laura tells him, imitating her mother, Joan. "It's either this or having her go buy them at Malarkey's." Malarkey's is the fancy French bakery where Laura worked the summers between her sophomore and senior years at college. She used to bring leftovers from the display case home after work for her mother—slices of gâteaux, tartes tatins, éclairs. Joan, who'd never had much of a sweet tooth, learned to love fancy pastry late in life, and Malarkey pies have been a Thanksgiving tradition for the past ten years.

"It was hard enough persuading her to let me make them. They'd better be perfect."

"And this is the most we can do?" Sam shakes his head. "Saving her buying pies."

Laura's mother went bankrupt three months ago. The dry

cleaner she bought with a small inheritance had been struggling
for years, losing ground to Korean competition. She sold the old
family home in the eighties, when the market was up, and moved
to a rented condo. She told Laura she'd buy a place again when
the market moved, but instead she put the money from the
house into the business, and now there's nothing left. She's still
in the condo, but her savings are running out, and she can't
touch her 401(k) for another five years without penalties.

"I know it's dumb," Laura says, climbing in beside her husband. "But Malarkey's was one of those little luxuries for her."

"Just remember," Sam says, patting her thigh, "love is not
a pie."

"Love is not a lot of things," she says, staring forward. "It's
not going into debt when you can't afford it to pay for our wedding and honeymoon, right? It's not pouring your money into
some stupid failing business for years. It's not sitting around
for a decade in a rented condo in Paramus when you could
have bought a house and had some fucking equity. It's not
lying about your finances and pretending everything's fine and
refusing help until there's no money left." She pauses to take a
jagged breath. "If I had a fucking dime for everything love isn't,
we wouldn't be in this jam."

"We can help her," Sam says quietly, keeping his eyes on the
road. Sam's in his first semester as an assistant professor of English, after five years of grad school working on Jane Austen and
two as an adjunct, and despite his student loans and uncertain
tenure he's feeling like a man again after having Laura support
him for the last few years. She was a pastry chef in Berkeley, but
since they moved back east for his job, she's only been able to get
mornings at a local bakery. Her hands are shiny and scabbed

with the countless careless little burns she picks up around the ovens.

"I know it's scary," he says. "But try not to think of it as something we're being forced to do. It's our choice. We're going to do the right thing."

"It may be a choice for you," she says. "She's not your mother."

He wants to tell her, *And you're my wife*. Instead he sighs. "All I'm saying is, we can help. We will. You just have to talk to her, tell her she has to let us help now, not later, when everything's gone. With what she has left she can make a down payment on a place, and we can stretch to cover her mortgage and ours, and then at least she won't be losing money on rent." He doesn't mention the possibility of Laura's mother's finding a new job. She has skills, they tell her. Look at the great job she did with Laura's wedding dress. What about bridal work? She's been sending out résumés for months, but with less and less hope, until now, they know, in a gesture both defiant and despairing, she doesn't even include a cover letter. She spends her days at home in a nubbly armchair, breaking the spines of cheap paperbacks, waiting for the phone to ring.

"I'm sorry," Laura says, blotting her eyes with the heel of her hand.

"Anyway, you know me," he tells her, "genetically predisposed toward filial obligation."

Sam is Indian. When Laura first brought him home to visit her mother, she warned her on the phone. "Indian?" her mother said. "Really?" "I think I'd know," Laura replied, laughing. "Only," her mother said, "you don't mean he's black? You can tell me. I'd prefer to know." The first time he came for Thanksgiving, Joan asked Sam if he liked turkey and he told her, "Are you kidding? Especially the white meat."

"At least your parents have a house that they own," Laura tells him now, "and enough money in the bank to take care of themselves. God, how can you stand to have married into this?"

"It's tough," he says gently, signaling for their exit. "The sex helps."

•

Laura's Aunt Marilyn and her Uncle Phil are at the condo already when they arrive. Uncle Phil is watching the game, a gin and tonic in hand. He has fifty bucks on the Pack to upset Dallas, he tells them when they walk in. Dallas, Sam sees, setting a pie down on the counter, is already up by two touchdowns. Laura, a dish in each hand, lets her mother hug her, balancing her offerings carefully. When she lifts the foil off them, condensation drips onto the pastry of the apple pie. The tips of the meringue are a little flattened, but her mother tells her they look gorgeous.

"How are you?" Laura asks, and Joan tells her briskly, "Fine, fine."

Pretty soon the whole family is there, including Laura's sister, Suzy, the waitress, and her boyfriend, Derek, who beat her once (that they know of). These are the ways Sam thinks of his in-laws. Derek, whose hairline's been receding, has recently shaved his head. Suzy keeps stroking his pale skull, and Derek even dips his head for Joan to feel it. "Oh," she says, laughing. "Smooth as a baby's behind." But then her fingers stop and Derek stands up quickly. "That's a scar from when I fell off a bike when I was six," he says. He'd forgotten all about it until it appeared after shaving. There's another, he shows them, just above his ear, where he got cut in a fight with his father. "It's the old man's ring." Suzy stands on tiptoe and kisses the spot, then rubs the lipstick off.

Laura's cousin Nick — Marilyn and Phil's eldest — and his wife, Candy, are the last to arrive. Nick's the one who spent some time in juvy for breaking and entering. Now he's a legal aide in the city. They have their son, Bobby, with them, three years old, blond, unbelievably cute. Nick has just moved the family to Brooklyn from Lolita. "Lower Little Italy," Bobby explains to everyone loudly. "*Low*-li-ta. Get it? Lo-*lee*-ta. Lo-li-*tah!*" They have more space than in their old apartment, Nick explains, for a lot less. "Which is good," he tells Laura, "because this little guy — clothes, food, T.O.Y.S." — he glances from Bobby to Candy, who is trying to take his jacket — is E.X.P.E.N.*sive*."

No one mentions Sam's job, although it's the first time he's seen the family since he took it in May, and he feels ridiculous for caring, for envying Nick and Candy the attention lavished on Bobby. He opens a beer for himself.

Sam tries to talk to Suzy and Derek for a few minutes, but they seem on the verge of a fight about what she's wearing — a little black dress, as if for a cocktail party — and pretty soon Derek, scalp flushed, joins Uncle Phil on the couch, both of them leaning forward, concentrating on the game, which is not even close but demands all their attention to hear over the conversation behind them. Sam perches on the arm of the sofa and watches with them. He says something about Favre, and Uncle Phil looks around and smiles and tells him for the third year in a row, "I didn't know you liked football." Next Sam tries to chat with Nick and Candy, but Aunt Marilyn wants to show Candy the sweater she's knitting for Bobby, and Nick volunteers to carve the turkey for Joan. (He says it's a good-sized bird and she tells him it ought to be, she asked for the one that laid the golden eggs.) Which leaves Suzy and Laura, who demands, as soon as they're alone, to know why Suzy didn't bring anything. "Joan's got it covered," Suzy says. "There's always too much food anyway." But Laura tells her that's not the point. She could at least have brought some wine. "Jesus," Suzy says. "Who died and made you Mom?"

Sam ends up with Bobby, which is fine by him, and the two of them, after some formalities, start to crawl around the dining table, Sam growling and Bobby laughing and running behind the chairs. Sam stops for a second to grab a paper cup off the counter and grip it in his teeth so it covers his mouth and nose like a muzzle. "Here," he growls through his teeth, "comes the Schnuffulupulus," and Bobby shrieks and ducks beneath the chairs, where Sam is careful not to catch him. Sam hasn't seen the boy for six months, and he's amazed at how much he's changed. Nick comes over and joins in, but after a moment he reaches under the table and pulls Bobby out and pins him, bearing down and rubbing his whiskers on his son's face while Sam looks on. "Surrender?" he cries. "Surrender?" Sam wonders what the boy smells like close up.

Laura's mother nudges her as they look on from the kitchenette.

"What?"

"See?" Joan says.

"See what?"

"Laura," she says, with a show of impatience. "Somebody would make a great father. What are you two waiting for?"

"Mother, do you mind?" Laura pulls over a stack of napkins and begins folding them into fans.

Joan leans over the stove, lifts the lid on the mashed potatoes, stirs the gravy. It is a mild obsession with her that everything be ready at exactly the same time.

"I mean" — Joan drops her voice — "is there a problem? You know they say you shouldn't stay on the pill for too long. It's not good for you."

"There's no problem." *And if there were I wouldn't tell you,* Laura thinks. Mention of the pill makes her imagine her mother rooting through her bag.

"Because I'd love to be a grandmother while I'm still young enough to enjoy my grandchildren. Look at Marilyn."

"Don't hold your breath."

"I'm not holding my breath, Laura. I just think you two should think about it. You're thirty-four. Kids are the best thing in the world. You guys changed my life, you know, gave it a whole new meaning."

Laura's father left when she and Suzy were still in middle school. For the first day or two, after all the fighting, it was silent. Her mother would run the dishwasher half full just for the noise. He kept in touch, bought them occasional lavish gifts, never paid any support, and their mother, who hadn't worked for ten years, went out and found what she could, mostly in those first few years as a seamstress. Laura knows how hard she worked to support them. She remembers taking her mother's hand once to cross the street, how Joan winced, turning it over and seeing her thumb purple and pimpled with scabs where she had pricked herself.

"Our lives have enough meaning right now. If anyone needs meaning, you should talk to Suze."

Her mother looks at the gravy again, watching it run off the wooden spoon.

"I didn't mean that," Laura says. Suzy has had two abortions, both of which Joan has paid for. Her mother just shakes her head.

"All I'm trying to say is that I love Sam. You know I could use some good news right now."

"Mom, we're not even sure we want a kid," Laura says. "Or if we could afford one yet." She pauses, fusses with the final napkin. "I mean timewise. With Sam's new job and me looking. It's just bad timing right now."

"Oh!" The pan is boiling over. Joan turns off the burner, its hiss fluttering and then still. She tastes the gravy gingerly, pursing her lips. "Scorched," she says.

Laura realizes that even though they've only just got here, she's not going to be able to talk about money with her mother today. She feels a resignation very close to relief. She keeps watching her husband as Joan takes the napkins out to the table.

Aunt Marilyn comes up beside her and nudges her in the ribs. "They're cute, aren't they?" Laura nods. "How's she doing? Your mother?" Marilyn asks, and Laura tells her, "Fine." Then, "We're going to look out for her, okay?"

Sam has finally realized that Bobby wants to be caught and has him in a hug.

"You know she'd do the same for you if the situation were reversed," Marilyn says, and Laura nods slowly. "Of course, you do anything for your own kids."

"You know how the Schnuffulupulus got his name?" Sam asks Bobby, and the little boy shakes his head seriously.

"You're a good daughter," Marilyn says after a second. "A credit to your mom." And Laura wonders whom she's praising.

"Be*cause*," Sam says, pouncing, "he loves to snuffle up to you." He presses his head to the little boy's belly, nuzzles him, then plays dead while Bobby clambers over him.

Laura nods to where Bobby and Sam are wrestling on the floor.

"I should go and rescue my husband from your grandson," she says.

Bobby is sitting on Sam's chest, asking where he's from. "Where I'm from?" Sam says thoughtfully. "Well, let's see." He starts to draw a map in the air before him. "If this is your house" — he points to an invisible spot under Bobby's nose — "and this is where we are right now, then I must live right *here*." And he pokes the little boy in his belly, tickles him until, wailing with laughter, Bobby squirms free. But only into the arms of Laura, who grabs an ankle — "How about here?" — and proceeds to tickle his foot.

"No, really," Bobby says, finally breaking away from them both. He's panting, and the fine pale hair at his neck and temples is dark and stuck to his head. Sam finally tells him that they're from New Haven. Bobby wants to know if he can visit and Laura grins, says, "Sure."

"And when it's time for you to go to college, you can come and live with us if you like," Sam tells him. And as he says it, just for a second he can see it. Him and Laura, years from now, welcoming Bobby on their porch. He'll come by for Laura's home cooking, Sam's beer.

Bobby squeals in delight and runs to tell his mom that Sam says he can come live with them.

"Oh really?" she says, and Laura calls quickly, "When he goes to college."

"Oh, when you're a *Yale* man," Candy says, and laughs, and Sam sees her relief, sees it's a joke. The idea of her son at Yale is flattering but ludicrous to her, and for a second Sam feels his heart contract. He felt it when he saw Nick wrestling with his son. It occurs to him, *This kid won't even like me in a couple of years.*

He turns to Laura and shrugs. "Neat kid."

"You want?" she asks him quietly.

"You?" he says. They look at each other for a long moment, and then behind them Laura's mother calls, "All right, everyone."

Suzy sits and watches as her mother and Laura carry food to the table. "This is great," she says, "just one day in the year to have someone wait on me. God, I hate that job. You want to trade, Mom?"

Laura leans over and tells her, "Not funny, Suze."

"Screw you, Laur," Suzy whispers back, grinning, as Joan carries the bird to the table.

"Ta-da!"

"Look at that," Marilyn says. "This is great, sis. Next year you'll have to come to us. All of you."

"I don't see why," Joan says, smiling stiffly. "We've been having Thanksgiving here for years."

"Just for a change," Marilyn says quickly. "To give you a break."

"I don't want a break," Joan tells her. "And I don't need to be told to quit when I'm ahead."

There's silence for a moment—Laura sees the wrinkles around her mother's mouth harden into two deep lines running vertically from the corners of her mouth to her chin—and then Uncle Phil says, "That's one big bird," and Bobby cries, "Big

Bird!" and Phil says, "Uh-huh," and puts a piece in his mouth. "*Dee*licious."

Later, as the wine moves around the table, Nick starts up on the market. How they should all get in on it. How there's easy money to be made. "It's our middle-class duty, all right," Phil says, laughing, but Suzy says she's not middle-class. She's a waitress, she says, looking around the table. Derek's a mechanic. He nods. How's that middle-class? "While your Uncle Phil is digesting that foot in his mouth . . ." Marilyn starts, and Laura tries to help by adding that being middle-class isn't just about income. It's about background. Education. How you were brought up. She looks to her mother for help. She looks to Sam, but he doesn't want to get into it. His parents had a grocery and then a small restaurant when he was growing up. His father owned it and served in it for years. Nick says it all depends on how you define your terms. He sounds impatient with the discussion, but when Laura tries to drop it, he keeps after her to say what she means by middle-class. "You know what I mean," she tells him, and he says, "*You* don't even know what you mean." And finally Sam steps in.

"I suppose for us, me and Laura, it means knowing for the first time we could go to pretty much any restaurant in town." He smiles sheepishly, his face already flushed from one beer. "Not that we do, of course. And it means that too, I guess. It means having more than enough and not quite enough at the same time. Counting our lucky stars," he says, "and counting our pennies."

Candy gives a little laugh, but Nick is looking at him as if he's a stranger. As if he's never heard his voice, and that gives Sam a moment of pleasure. He recognizes it as the same kick he gets when a class is going well, when he remembers how much he cares about his subject even if his undergrads don't. But when he looks around to share it with Laura, he sees she's looking stricken too. She excuses herself to fetch the pies. For a moment there is just the tick of flatware on china. Then Marilyn tells him politely, "That's really interesting," and something in her tone pushes Sam on.

"It is," he says. "It's all about choosing, really. Being middle-class. Not just choosing something, but choosing something *instead* of something else. A new car or a nicer house. A sofa or a vacation. Which is the terrible thing, of course. They're all different. Like apples and oranges. So how do you choose if they're not the same?"

Too late he realizes he's lecturing, shrugs in embarrassment, runs out of steam. They watch Laura lay her pies on the table one by one, with infinite care. It sounds like a rhetorical question, but it isn't. Sam doesn't expect an answer, doesn't have one. He poses questions like this at school, and his students never know if they should attempt a reply or if the answer is so self-evident they can't see it. And sometimes in those pauses Sam himself wonders if he even wants an answer, if he doesn't just prefer the question, poised, immaculate.

There's the same stillness over the table now, all of them staring at their plates for a clue, until Joan says, "Money. That's how." She puts a hand over Sam's, squeezes. "They're not equal, those things. They can't be. But money makes them seem so." She nods her head once, decisively, smiles blindly around the table.

"So who's for pie?" Laura raises her knife and points at each in turn. "Apple cinnamon, lemon meringue, pumpkin." And Uncle Phil says he can't choose; he'll take a sliver of each.

•

Before they leave, Joan carves slice after slice of cold turkey breast, wraps them in foil. She gives the package to Laura, who begins to decline. "Full," she says, patting her stomach.

"For Sam," Joan tells her. "He loves my turkey."

"Mom," Laura tries. But then she knows they'll help her mother, just knows it. And Joan will let them. They'll do everything in their power, whatever it takes, and suddenly there's nothing else to say, nothing to discuss — Laura isn't even sure if they're being selfless or selfish. "Thanks," she says.

"Happy Thanksgiving, darling."

When Sam sees the foil parcel, he smiles glumly. "See?" he says, pulling out of the drive. "Love is a sandwich."

"Yeah?" she says. "Maybe." Something is coming back to her. Childhood mornings when she was just a toddler, before Suzy was born, squeezing into the bed between her parents. "Making sandwiches," they used to call it.

"Jesus," she says softly. She stares out at the skyline floating past in the distance, like the fingers of a reaching hand. Her heart is racing and she finds herself crying again. Sam, never taking his eyes off the road, slows down, cups the clenched fist in her lap in his own hand, steers them carefully over the GW Bridge.

•

At home, in bed, they read silently before sleep. It has rained on the way back, pattering through the leaves, and now water drips off the gutters above them, the windowsill, the tree outside, the drips coming in odd, uneven rhythms like a host of slightly unsynchronized clocks. Sam sets his book down and presses against Laura. Her forearm is exposed and he runs his face along it, smelling her skin. "What are you doing?" she asks, annoyed, and he explains innocently, "Schnuffling." He plucks with his lips at the down on her arm. "Grazing."

He slips his hand under her old sweatshirt, finds she's still wearing her bra. He snaps the elastic of a strap gently until she tells him to stop, but in a soft whiny voice that makes him continue. He slides his hands inside her bra and she wriggles over onto her side, still pretending to read.

"Booby," he says, his fingers cupping her breast. He squeezes gently, lifts her bra over her breasts, puts his lips to her ear. "If you love somebooby," he breathes, and she starts to giggle. "Set them free." And she starts to turn toward him as he croons, "Free, free, set them free."

"Cakes of baby?" she says in his arms. "Pie of honey?"

Afterward they lie together, she draped over him, her head cradled against his chest, a position they both love yet only find comfortable after sex.

"Hubster," she says, and he says, "Hmm?"

"Hub-a-lub," she says, and he says, "What?"

"Hub-a-licious," she says, and he says, getting it at last, "Wifey."

Outside, the dripping has slowed to a single slow beat, and in the silence they squeeze each other tight, clenching until they can barely breathe, until their joints pop, until they're finally sure nothing can ever come between them.

TODAY IS SUNDAY

O N SUNDAY I visit my father, the first time since Christmas, and he tells me my timing's bad. He's off to visit his own mother in hospital.

My grandmother's senile, eighty-eight, hasn't recognized anyone for donkey's years, but he still drives the thirty miles to the hospital once or twice a week. He slipped a disk last winter climbing a ladder, and he has a pinched nerve in his back that can double him over. It's bothering him now as he looks for his shoes. He clutches his side with one hand and winces, but when I ask him if he's okay, he says it's nothing.

"It doesn't look like nothing."

"Old age," he says, as if it's a war wound, and gives a little groan.

"Oh, great."

I try telling him it's pouring out and the forecast is for sleet. I ask him to give it a miss this week. I'll make lunch (he pulls a face). There's footy on the box. But this is a mistake. He won't put himself first. The old lady, I tell him at last, won't even notice, and he looks at me as if I'm a stranger.

"I was just thinking of you," I say quickly. "Christ. Am I not allowed to care?"

He pinches the seams of his trouser legs, tugs them up an inch as he sits to put on his shoes.

"There's a difference between caring," he says, pulling his laces tight, "and carrying on."

I stand over him for a moment. His hair, what's left of it, is salt-and-peppery, but when he straightens up I see his stubble is coming in pure white.

"At least let me drive you," I say, and he tells me, "Suit yourself."

I make him sit in the back so he can stretch out a bit, and he asks if I'm his bloody chauffeur now. The idea tickles him. He calls me James. Puts on the plummy voice. Gives me a wave like the Queen Mum when I ask him if he's comfy. The whole bit. In the mirror, I watch him light a cigarette. He's supposed to have given up. Doctor's orders. Ages ago. I haven't seen him smoke in maybe ten years. He catches me watching him and makes a face.

"Don't mind, do you?" he says, and I tell him, "Oh, no. Course not. Be my guest."

"Champion. Only I remember when you was a lad," he says, taunting now. "You used to make a big song and dance about me smoking. You thought your old dad'd drop dead any second."

"I was a kid," I say. I watch him in the mirror as he takes another drag. He puts his fingers to his lips, palm in, and removes the cigarette. It's a gesture I haven't seen since childhood.

"Asked you once what you wanted for Christmas and you said for me to give up. Proper whiner, you were."

"Crack the window, would you?" I say. "It was for your own good."

He taps his ash on the window frame and shakes his head. "Selfish," he says. "Spoiled."

"Did Mum know?" My mother, who died three years ago.

"Did she heck."

"So what d'you do? Drive out here each week and have a smoke?"

"I think I deserve it," he says.

The car thuds over the compression plates of a bridge.

At a traffic light, I turn to him and say, "Give us one, then."

He doesn't know I smoke. Since school. I think of us now, before I left home, both sneaking them on the sly under my mother's nose. No wonder we never tumbled to each other.

"So that's how it is," he says bleakly. "Monkey see, monkey bleeding do."

I hold out my hand, but he just looks at it until the lights change.

"Drive on."

He blows smoke through his nostrils and smiles and for a moment he looks young again, the spitting image of the fellow in our old photo albums.

It makes me think of an afternoon in our back garden when I was little. A birthday party perhaps, summer, a bunch of kids, my mother, my gran. He had this trick of keeping a football in the air longer than anyone else. He'd just stand there on one foot, his thin hips swaying slightly, swinging his leg lazily back and forth like a pendulum, the ball popping up off his toes. I was dead proud of him. He looked as if he could go on forever. Still, it started to get boring after a bit. I wanted a turn — even better, I wanted him to teach me — but he just kept going as if he were setting some record. In the end, my grandmother called, "Give Paul a go, then," but he shook his head. He reached into his pocket and pulled out a packet of fags, drew one out, and lit it — all without losing control. He puffed away contentedly, grinning around the cig, eyes half closed against the smoke, until all of us were staring at the curving, trembling tip of ash.

•

I haven't been to the hospital for three years. It's a sprawling Victorian setup, half closed now that a new hospital's opened in town. The main building, with its crenellated clock tower, is perched on a hill overlooking landscaped gardens and rolling fields. The lawns are neat, but the flowerbeds are empty mounds of earth. When I was still living at home before college, my father taught me to drive out here. The quiet roads were good for practicing maneuvers—reversing round corners, three-point turns—but we still ended up in a shouting match every time I ground the gears or clipped the curb. He was always whinging that I took the speed bumps—"sleeping policemen," he called them—too fast, and I creep over them now.

The door to my grandmother's ward has two handles, one in the usual place, the other about a foot from the top. My father grasps both and turns them together.

Inside, we find her in a corner of the lounge, so shrunken and slumped I hardly recognize her. Her head lolls back against her chair, too heavy for her creased, deflated neck, and she peers at us damply from hooded eyes. We pull up chairs and my father takes her hand. He talks to her, just nonsense really, the noises you'd make to a baby, and while he talks he rubs her hand. When she drools a little, he wipes her face with his handkerchief. He tweaks her nose when he's done, and the old lady smiles vaguely. I look at her other hand, where it lies in her lap, but I don't take it.

I wish he wouldn't treat her like a child.

"Here," my father says to her. "How about a banana?" He pulls one like magic out of his pocket. It looks strange in the ward, bright and exotic, and I remember him telling me once they only had bananas for Christmas when he was a boy. He unpeels it carefully and offers it to her, but her eyes are unfocused. My father touches it to her lips, and when her mouth stays closed he rubs the tip of it back and forth — I want to tell him to leave her be — until she opens wide. Her lips close on it, sucking, and he twists it gently to break off a piece in her mouth. Slowly, absently, she begins chewing, and I look away.

There's a white board by the door for the nurses to write messages on. "Today is Sunday, March tenth," it says. "It is a cold, wet day."

"Promise me," my father says quietly, "if I ever get like this, you'll do me in. Knock me on the head or something."

He looks at me as if it's a dare, and I stare back at him.

"Oh, right," I tell him. "No bother." And then, "Do you ever wonder how it makes me feel, you asking that?"

"You'll thank me," he says with sudden heat. "You don't believe me? Listen." He lowers his voice. "I wish my mother would die. D'you hear me? I wish my own mother would die. How d'you think that makes me feel?"

He turns back to her and I watch him stroke her cheek. He calls her "pet," and she bends her head to his touch.

"Oh, stop looking so worried," he tells me, glancing over. "I'll be gone long before that. My old fella had a heart attack before he was fifty-five."

I called my father on his birthday last year and asked him how old he was and he told me sixty, and for a second I thought he was pulling my leg.

My grandmother has fallen asleep. Her head rolls, her mouth

falls open, and a ball of chewed banana drops onto her collar. My father picks it up daintily in his handkerchief, sees me watching, pretends to toss it my way. I flinch but don't smile.

"Why do you carry on, then?" I ask him. "Keep coming all these years?"

"Because." He shrugs and then, to her, he starts to sing very quietly, like out of *The Wizard of Oz*, "Becoz, becoz, becoz, becoz, be-*coz*. What else can I do?"

When he decided she couldn't get on by herself anymore, she came and lived with us for a few months, but she would forget where she was, get angry, storm out, get lost. He thought she'd walk through plate glass, burn the house down, get hit by a car. ("All the things I used to worry about happening to you when you were a youngster," he told me once.) When he first moved her here, he wouldn't let my mother or me visit for a couple of weeks.

"I just want a word with the nurses before we're off," he says now, getting up stiffly. "Keep an eye on her, eh?" I make as if to tip my chauffeur's cap, but I feel uneasy alone with her.

I remember a visit, eight years ago maybe, when I was still learning to drive. He told me to wait outside in the car — the old Cortina — while he settled her down and said goodbye. I watched him come out to the car in the rearview mirror. I remember seeing him struggling with the handles on the door and hurrying across the car park toward me. When he got in, he told me to get going. I still had to think about everything then: starting the engine, giving it gas, putting the car in first, balancing the clutch. When I was ready, I checked the mirror. There wasn't another car in sight, but I wanted to make all this second nature before the test. In the mirror, I saw my grandmother at the window of the ward. I thought for a second she was waving, and then I saw her hand turn white as it struck the glass.

"Come on," my father said tersely. "Stop faffing about."

I signaled, revved the engine, lifted the clutch, and stalled the car. The hand brake was still set.

"Fuck's sake."

I went through it all again. Put the car back in neutral. Turned the ignition again. This time I didn't look in the mirror, remembered to release the brake, but the car still jerked, roaring, out of the car park. "Of all the cack-handed . . ." My father pulled on the brake with a tearing sound and shoved me out so he could take over.

When I look up now, my grandmother is staring at me. She's breathing hoarsely, making sounds deep in her throat. I'm about to get a nurse when she says, "Don?" My father's name.

"He'll be right back, Gran," I tell her, raising my voice a little. I look away in the direction he's gone, but there's no sign of him, and when I look back she's still staring at me.

"Don?" she says again. "Donald?" And at last I take her hand and tell her, "Yeah." She falls back to sleep like that, her hand in mine. The skin is loose on her bones, wrinkled and liver-spotted but disconcertingly soft.

When my father comes back he asks me if I'm ready, and then he sees me holding her hand and he says we can stay a little while, so we do. We're silent, both a little embarrassed. She doesn't wake again, but we watch her chest rising and falling until we take our own breaths in time.

"Was she all right while I was gone?" he asks at last, and I nod. I don't know how to tell him what happened. Not without risking some clumsy hurt. The lie makes me feel as if I've cheated him, as if I owe him something, but at the same time sharply protective. I'm going to have to keep this secret, carry it until he dies, and the idea of outliving my father suddenly makes me feel old — older even than him.

•

Later in the car he says, "I didn't mean it before."

I look over at him.

"About putting me out of my misery and that."

"I hope not."

He reaches into his pocket for cigarettes.

"Would you pack that in if I asked you?" I say.

"Nah."

He rattles his box of matches.

"I couldn't have done it anyway."

He grins. "Think I'd have asked you otherwise?"

He lights up, and in the dusk his face flares briefly. It makes me think of the long nights as a kid when I was afraid to go to sleep in the dark, when he'd sit with me after he turned the lamp out, smoking so I'd know he was still there by the glow of the cigarette. We had a joke, something we'd seen on TV or read in a comic. When he turned the light off he'd put on a stern voice, strike a match below his chin, and intone, "The face of tomorrow . . . *today.*"

I see a pub on the way back and pull in.

"Want a bevvy?" I say, and he tells me, "Yeah, all right."

Inside, I ask him what he wants and he goes, "Pint of bitter." And then, "An' a short, eh? Since you're driving."

When I bring the drinks to the table, he's fishing his cigarettes out.

"You want?" he says, holding the pack out. There's one extended.

"Go on, then."

I watch him dip his head to light his, the gesture so familiar, and then he holds out his cupped hands and I bend my face to take the flame.

"Your health," he says, lifting his glass.

Afterward, he settles himself in the back seat and tells me, "Home, James."